P9-CSH-790

JUST FOR THE SUMMER

JUST FOR THE SUMMER

by CHRISTINE McDONNELL

PICTURES BY DIANE DE GROAT

Viking Kestrel

VIKING KESTREL
Viking Penguin Inc., 40 West 23rd Street, New York, New York 10010, U.S.A.
Penguin Books Ltd, 27 Wrights Lane, London W8 5TZ (Publishing & Editorial) and
Harmondsworth, Middlesex, England (Distribution & Warehouse)
Penguin Books Australia Ltd, Ringwood, Victoria, Australia
Penguin Books Canada Limited, 2801 John Street, Markham, Ontario, Canada L3R 1B4
Penguin Books (N.Z.) Ltd, 182-190 Wairau Road, Auckland 10, New Zealand

Text copyright © Christine McDonnell, 1987
Illustrations copyright © Diane de Groat, 1987
All rights reserved
First published in 1987 by Viking Penguin Inc.
Published simultaneously in Canada
Printed in the United States of America by The Book Press, Brattleboro, Vermont
Set in DeVinne
1   2   3   4   5   91   90   89   88   87

Library of Congress Cataloging-in-Publication Data
McDonnell, Christine.   Just for the summer.
Summary: Reunited for the summer, friends Emily, Ivy, and Lydia keep busy
at day camp, creating a toddler day care center, and other projects.
[1. Friendship—Fiction.   2. Summer—Fiction] I. De Groat, Diane, ill.   II. Title.
PZ7.M1543Ju 1987   [Fic]   87-8201 ISBN 0-670-80059-7

For SooAe

CONTENTS

JUST FOR THE SUMMER

SUMMER VISIT

"There she is! Lyd-i-a, Lyd-i-a, over here." Connie's voice sailed out above the airport crowd, drawing stares.

Lydia turned and spotted her aunts. May's helmet of gray-streaked hair stood out clearly; very tall and thin, she peered out over the heads of the crowd like a distinguished knight surveying the ranks. Connie stood next to her, waving her arms.

Lydia picked her way through the crowd and gave them each a hug. May tugged her braid. "Oh good! We've got you back for the whole summer."

Connie scouted the bags starting to fall out into the revolving bin.

"It's a red duffel," Lydia said. The bag fell out of the chute with a plop, landing upside down. Connie fished it out as it moved slowly by.

They passed the bag back and forth three times before they reached the car. Lydia climbed in the front seat between her aunts.

"Emily's jumping like a toad, she's so eager to see you," said Connie.

"We set the dollhouse up on a table in your room," May said. "We haven't let anybody touch it, not even Emily or that imp Ivy, even though they begged and begged. It's waiting for you just the way you left it."

Lydia pictured it. The dolls would be sitting in the living room, except for Cook in her rocker and the baby sleeping in the nursery. Had she left the Christmas decorations up? She'd spent much of her last visit making them with Emily. Decked out with holly, a tree, and presents, the dollhouse had looked like a miniature Christmas card.

As soon as they reached the house, Lydia headed upstairs. The dollhouse stood next to the window. The decorations were gone. She must have taken them down in January. The dolls were in place, just as she remembered. Mr. and Mrs. Higgins sat on the living room sofa, side by side. The children sat on the two armchairs, looking at each other. If their faces could move, the older sister would be sticking her tongue out at her brother.

Just then the doorbell rang and Emily bounded up the stairs, two at a time, eager as a puppy. She gave Lydia a quick hug, almost pushing her over. "You're back! I hoped you'd come back. We've got the whole summer. I'm sorry your father's sick again, though."

Lydia nodded, embarrassed. It was awkward every time someone mentioned his illness. "Thanks. It's okay. He's getting better." She tried to sound surer than she felt.

Emily rushed on. "Want to play badminton? I set up the net as soon as I heard you were coming."

"I only played once before."

"It's easy. You just hit the birdie." She pulled one out of her pocket. "It even has feathers. Tweet tweet."

The girls went downstairs, and Lydia stopped by the kitchen to say where she was going. May was slicing onions. Tears ran down her face as she worked.

"Aunt May, are you all right?" Lydia asked.

"It's just the onions. Have fun. I might come out later and challenge you both." She sopped up the tears with a paper towel and waved goodbye.

Lydia and Emily played until the shadow from the house covered the lawn.

"I better go in," Lydia said.

"I'll come over after breakfast. Let's play with the dollhouse."

Lydia waved goodbye and headed back through the trees to her aunts' house.

Dinner was her favorite, homemade pizza. As they ate, the aunts described their adventures in Greece during spring vacation. Since they both taught at a small college just outside of town, they had vacations free for travel. May taught math and Connie taught history.

Aunt Connie told stories with big arm gestures and dramatics.

"We ended up in a tiny fishing village just before dinner. The inn was smaller than our kitchen, with one bedroom upstairs. They brought us a loaf of hot bread and bowls of stew, tasty, but very chewy. We had no idea what was in it.

"So at the end of the meal your Aunt May looked up a few words in the dictionary and asked the owner what it was. He took a little stub of a pencil from behind his ear and began to draw on the napkin. First a round head, then one long curved thing. Then another. Well, by the time he drew in the third tentacle, my poor stomach began to twist and turn."

More stories followed as the aunts tried to outdo one another. Lydia laughed so much she forgot all about her mother and father until Aunt Connie suggested she call home to say she'd arrived safely.

"Have fun and don't forget to help," her mother said over the phone. "May and Connie have their own work to do, you know. And for heaven's sake, stop worrying. Who's the mother and who's the daughter in this family, anyway?'' They always joked about that. Her parents said that Lydia was more practical than either of them.

Lydia put a goodnight kiss on the receiver before she hung up.

''I wish they were here,'' she told her aunts as they sat on the porch counting fireflies.

Later, lying in her bed, she couldn't fall asleep. She tossed and turned, mangling the sheets until finally she had to get up and straighten the tangle. Then she lay with her arms folded behind her head and tried not to move at all.

Soft and vague, her aunts' voices drifted up from the porch. Finally they came upstairs to bed. Aunt May hummed in the bathroom. Then Aunt Connie clicked off the hall lights and turned on the radio in her room. Lydia could hear only fragments of the music, not the full melody.

After a while the music stopped and the house was still. But Lydia was still wide awake.

She climbed out of bed, tiptoed across the room and knelt in front of the open window. From her bedroom window at home, she could see a line of houses, each one just like the next, with little square yards in back, and TV antennas jutting up from the roofs. But here the window looked out onto a maple tree with thick leaves whispering in the breeze. Through the branches, Lydia spied Emily's house. A

light shone in the front bedroom. Someone else was still awake.

The big tree reminded Lydia of her father. When their house back home was built, the developer left only a few bushes in the yard.

"What a fool! He cut down the trees," her father said. "So what if the tree took a hundred years to grow? Dig it up, move it out. Now look at it. No shade and no place for birds."

He had bought new trees, skinny saplings with roots wrapped in burlap: maple, beech, linden, a line of birches along the back edge of the yard. At first they looked more like sticks than trees. He cared for them like babies, feeding them special fertilizer mixtures and watering them just enough and not too much, so that they grew tall and filled out. Someday they'd be as tall as the houses, or maybe even taller.

Who's taking care of the trees now? Lydia wondered. Mom won't remember, not with working and going to the hospital every day to visit. The trees need extra water to make it through the summer. Mom should've let me stay.

Finally her eyelids drooped. She yawned. What a long day! She'd started out back home, taken a plane all by herself, and now here she was in a different place altogether. She climbed back into bed and lay in the darkness for a few minutes listening to the wind whisper in the tree.

The next morning Emily rang the doorbell just as Lydia was finishing breakfast.

"I hope I'm not too early," she said, taking the last muffin off the plate.

"If we're up, you're not too early," Aunt Connie said.

Emily helped Lydia rinse the plates and load the dishwasher. "Let's play with the dollhouse," she said.

Lydia led the way upstairs. The dollhouse stood on the little table, waiting for them.

Emily peered into every room. "It's just like I remembered." She picked up the hand-cranked Victrola and put it to her ear as if she could hear its music.

Whenever Lydia played with the dollhouse she thought of her aunts and her mother playing with it when they were little girls. Even her grandmother had played with it.

"Let's rearrange the furniture," Emily suggested, "and write a list of new stuff to make." Emily was always organized.

The list got longer and longer: new rugs, bunk beds, a swing, new pictures for the parlor walls.

"Did your aunts tell you about the August fair?" Emily asked. "It's great! There are contests and rides and booths, and lots of ribbons to win. Everybody enters something."

"Like what?"

"Vegetables, animals, cakes and pies, anything you

make or grow. I'm going to enter something from my part of the garden, whichever vegetable does the best this summer."

"I don't have anything to enter," said Lydia.

"You'll think of something."

Just then, Aunt Connie called upstairs, "It's too nice to play inside all day. Let's go to the lake. I'll pack a picnic."

"Can we take the dollhouse people?" Emily asked Lydia.

Lydia wrapped them in a towel and packed them carefully in the bottom of her knapsack. She took the parents, Mr. and Mrs. Higgins, and the two older children, Martha and William.

"The cook and the baby should stay home. Cook can make supper and have it ready for the others when they get back," she said.

"Poor Cooky," said Emily.

"We'll make her a special treat sometime," Lydia said. "A party."

"Other cooks could come," Emily suggested.

"They'll make cake together."

"Like *In the Night Kitchen.*"

"But they'll eat it all themselves," said Lydia.

"Come on, you two," Aunt Connie called.

She drove them out to the lake, then planted her canvas chair on the sand at the far edge of the swim area where it was less crowded and better for reading. After a swim, she settled down with her book, a wide straw hat tilted over her eyes.

Lydia and Emily, left to themselves, spread their towels by the rocks that rimmed the cove. First they let the family have a picnic. Mr. Higgins lay back with his legs crossed. He looked a little silly in his dark suit. Mrs. Higgins sat primly upright; her body was hard to bend. The children leaned against a piece of rock.

"They want to go climbing," Emily said.

"Make them go on ahead. The parents won't know where they've gone," said Lydia.

Emily moved the dolls up the rock face. Reaching as high as she could, she settled both into a crack. "Make the mother look for them," she said.

Lydia got Mrs. Higgins to her feet. "Where are those children? They were here just a minute ago. Charles, dear. Charles! Wake up! The children have disappeared."

Lydia lowered her voice, making Emily giggle. "Disappeared? Don't be foolish, dear. They must have wandered off. Call them back."

Then in a higher voice again, she said, "Children, where are you? Chil-dren!"

"Now what happens?" Lydia asked in her own voice.

"Make the father climb the rocks," Emily suggested.

Lydia moved him up the side of the boulder, pausing at cracks and ledges.

"Oh, do be careful," she warned in Mrs. Higgins's

high, nervous voice.

"Be quiet, dear. I'm trying to concentrate," said Mr. Higgins.

"Make the children call out so he knows where they are," said Lydia.

Emily called, "Help, Father. We're over here. We can't get down."

The little father doll inched his way across the steep rock. "Stay where you are," he said. "Don't move one bit."

"How are we going to get them down?" Lydia asked.

"Let the father go first and tell them where to put their feet," Emily instructed.

Back on the safe sand, the father scolded. "Never do that again. You were lucky this time."

"Because you came and rescued us," said the girl doll.

"That's what fathers are for," Lydia made Mr. Higgins say. She stared at the little figure in her hand before putting him back on the blanket.

Emily watched her, embarrassed that the subject of fathers had come up.

"Day camp starts Monday," Emily said, changing the subject.

"Are you going?"

She nodded. "You are too. My mother told your aunts about it and they signed you up."

"They haven't said anything yet, but I only just got here," Lydia said. "What's it like?"

"You swim and go on trips. If we get a good counselor, it'll be fun."

That night, before bed, Lydia wrote to her father. She'd promised to write at least once a week. Her mother had typed the address on an index card. Riverside Hospital. It didn't look like a hospital to Lydia, since people wore regular clothes and went out for walks all over the grounds. But she knew it was a research hospital, and even though some people were strong enough to go out walking, others who weren't responding as well to treatment were lying in bed or sitting in wheelchairs. If her father, Mike, responded to the new medicine, then he'd be out walking on the lawn, too, and maybe he'd be coming home soon.

Hi, Dad,

The airplane ride was easy. No bumps. It's not as hot here as at home, maybe because of all the trees. Outside my window is a huge maple. I bet it's one hundred years old. I think it's a maple from the leaf. I didn't bring our tree book, but I'm pretty sure.

I went to the beach with Emily and Aunt Connie. We played with the dollhouse people. I'm going to day camp on Monday. Emily and Ivy are going too, so I guess it will be fun.

I hope the medicine's working and your roommate is nice. I'll write and tell you about camp.

XXXXXXXOOOOOOOO—(kisses and hugs),
Lydia

DAY CAMP
DISASTERS

At breakfast on Sunday, Aunt May explained, ''We didn't have a chance to ask you about camp but we went ahead with it because Emily was going. We only signed you up for the first session. Two weeks. Do you mind? We thought it might be fun, at least for a while.''

''I'll try it,'' Lydia said. ''If I don't like it, I'll quit.''

''I hated camp myself,'' Aunt Connie sniffed. ''Too organized.''

''It might be fun,'' Lydia said.

''Ivy's going too,'' Aunt May said.

''Heaven help the counselor!'' said Aunt Connie.

On Monday Lydia walked to camp with Emily. She carried her bathing suit and towel rolled up together and held by a rubber band. Her lunch was in a brown paper bag. Emily had a beach bag with blue and green fish on it.

"I went for a month last year," Emily said. She was kicking a round black stone, trying to get it all the way to the playground. When they crossed the big street by the library, the stone rolled into the sewer.

Ivy was waiting for them at the gate of the playground. "Hi, Lydia! Welcome back. Emily, guess who's here? Leo and Johnny! They're in the Rangers. We're Chickadees. Isn't that a dumb name!"

Just then a whistle blew and everyone in the playground funneled into the big gym. Lydia followed Emily and Ivy into the noisy hall. On the right side, where the girls' groups were gathering, they spotted the Chickadee sign.

"It *is* a dumb name," Lydia agreed with Ivy, who was right in front of her as they threaded single file through the crowd. "But it's better than the Woodpeckers." She pointed to the name of the next group over.

"Why are the girls all called stuff like Bluebirds and Robins? Why can't we be Eagles or Vultures or Buzzards?" Ivy asked. "Or Penguins. I wouldn't mind being a Penguin." She began to waddle, holding her arms stiff by her sides.

The Chickadees' counselor sat cross-legged on the floor beside the sign. When she smiled, her braces gleamed. But she didn't smile much. She looked as if she'd rather be somewhere else. "Miss Linda" her name tag read. She made red checks on her clipboard when they told her their names.

Maybe her braces hurt, Lydia thought.

When everyone had arrived, Miss Linda told them the plans. "First we go out to the field and play games. Then there's kickball until lunch. We eat back here. After lunch we'll hike to the pool and cool off," she said.

Lydia left her lunch bag next to Emily's and followed the crowd into the hot sun.

Sitting in another circle, this time on the grass, the Chickadees made up name chants.

"Annie, Annie, Bo Bany, Fee Fi Fo Fannie, An-nie."

"Emily, Emily, Bo Bemily, Fee Fi Fo Femily, Em-ly."

"Pat, Pat, Bo Bat, Fee Fi Fo Fat, Pa-at."

"Lydia, Lydia, Bo Bidia, Fee Fi Fo Fidia, Lyd-ia."

Then they played Cookie Jar, then another game with gestures.

"Kickball, main field," called the camp director, a chubby woman with a baseball cap and a whistle around her neck.

"I'd like to lie down under that tree over there,"

said Ivy, panting and pink in the face.

"When's lunch?" Lydia asked.

"Half an hour more. At least then we get to sit inside. The floor's good for jacks. Did you bring any?" Ivy asked.

"I did," said Emily.

"Shake a leg, girls," called Miss Linda. She was sitting in the shade by the side of the field, fanning herself with her sun visor.

Finally the whistle blew for lunch. The campers crowded into the main hall. Emily and Ivy found their lunches right away, but Lydia's bag was missing.

"I put it right next to yours," she said to Emily.

"Tell Miss Linda."

Miss Linda only said, "Look again." She didn't even get up to help.

Lydia walked around the edge of the auditorium. Her stomach rumbled. She wished she could go home to her aunts right now. Finally, in a corner next to some volleyballs, she spotted her lunch bag. Aunt Connie had written LYDIA in black marker. The egg salad sandwich was squished flat and someone had stolen her brownie. Even her plum had a gaping bite in its side.

Blinking back tears, Lydia found her way back to the Chickadees and sat down.

Ivy handed her a container of chocolate milk and a straw. "They gave these out while you were gone."

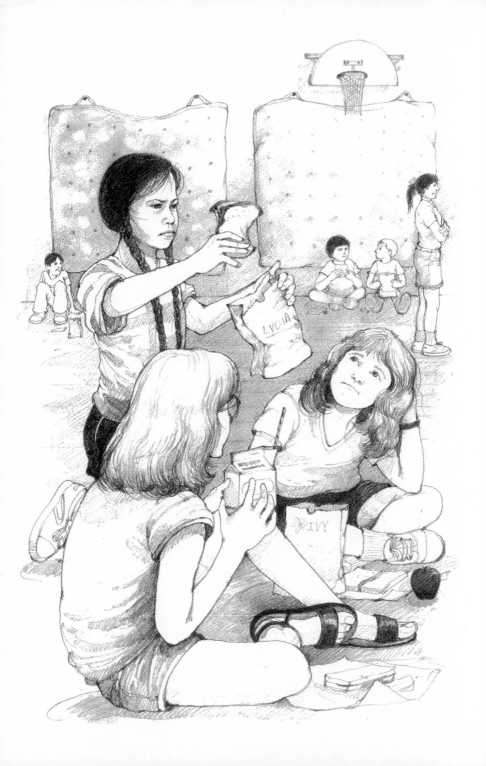

"Somebody stole my brownie and wrecked my sandwich." Lydia showed her friends.

"Yuk," said Emily. "Throw it out." She offered Lydia half of her sandwich. "Peanut butter and mint jelly."

"Mint jelly?"

"I don't like grape."

Lydia took a bite. She was so hungry that she didn't care what she ate. But she spluttered when she sipped the milk. Warm from standing too long, it was thick as medicine.

Lydia wiped her mouth. "How long before we go home?"

"About three more hours," Emily said.

"Cheer up. We're going swimming now," said Ivy.

At least we'll cool off, Lydia thought. She was still hungry.

"Stay together, Chickadees. We're after the Blue-birds. I don't want any strays," Miss Linda said.

Lydia felt like sticking out her tongue.

To reach the pool, they had to climb log steps winding back and forth up a steep hill. The air was muggy. Thick, scratchy bushes crowded the sides of the path, hiding places for the clouds of mosquitoes that bit their arms and legs and whined in their ears.

Finally, at the top of the hill, the pool gleamed bright turquoise through the fence. After they passed through the turnstile, a girl handed them each a metal locker key on a white elastic band that fit on a wrist or ankle.

Emily led the way into the girls' locker room. They changed quickly. Lydia felt embarrassed for a second, but everyone else was changing too. She pulled on her green tank suit and locked her clothes in the rusty metal locker.

Outside, the Chickadees gathered around Miss Linda, who sat on her towel by the edge of the shallow section. She was spreading suntan oil over her bulky legs.

She's going to sit on that towel all afternoon, Lydia thought. She won't even stick a toe in the water.

"Stay in the shallow end. If you pass the swimming test next week, you can go into the deep end and use the diving board." Miss Linda waved away their complaints. "That's the rule. That's just the way it is," she said.

Lydia, Emily and Ivy headed toward the other side of the pool where they wouldn't smell Miss Linda's coconut suntan oil.

"The shallow end for a week?" Ivy fumed. "I hate her."

Emily tried to be cheerful. "We can play shark. Or swim underwater. Or we could practice our swimming."

"I hate camp," said Ivy. She kicked the water angrily, making high splashes that sparkled in the sun.

Lydia and Emily copied her, trying to kick the water higher and higher. They began to giggle, then to laugh until they couldn't stop, churning the water and soaking everyone near them.

"Hey, you three sillies," Miss Linda called. "Calm down. You're acting like nuts."

"Three sillies, she called us," Ivy said, still giggling. She crossed her eyes and stuck out her tongue. One hand was on her hip, the other on her head. "I'm the first silly."

"Second," called Emily, stretching her mouth with her fingers as she bent her knees out and wiggled her behind.

Lydia hesitated for only a moment. "Third," she said. She tied her braids under her chin like a beard, pulled her ears out to the sides and blew up her cheeks like balls.

Tuesday, the second day of camp, was hot and muggy again. They went swimming in the morning. Even this early in the day, the water was lukewarm. The concrete was cold, though, and shadows from the trees around the fence left only a small patch of sun to sit in. Miss Linda and the other counselors spread their towels there.

When she was changing in the damp dressing room, Lydia dropped her underpants into a puddle on the floor. She fished them out quickly but they were wet and gray from the dirty water. She had to wear her shorts with nothing underneath and she worried all afternoon that someone would notice.

Lydia, Ivy and Emily stuck together all day. Miss Linda kept on calling them the three sillies. Three was a good number for friends as long as two didn't gang up on the other, and it was a perfect number for jacks. They played again on the smooth floor of the big hall. Emily and Ivy each had a set with dark gray solid metal jacks and a smooth red ball.

"Don't get those plastic jacks," Emily warned. "They're too light. They don't fall right when you throw them, and they're hard to catch. Get the good kind."

Lydia nodded. She planned to ask her aunts that evening. She had money that her mother had given her.

When Lydia got home from camp, there was a letter on the hall table, a blue envelope dotted with tiny white stars, like the sky at night but not as dark. She recognized her mother's writing and checked to see if it had a hint of her perfume. But it smelled only of paper and glue.

Her mother had printed the letter so Lydia would have no trouble reading it. Her script usually spilled forward with each letter crowding the next, as if the letters had tipped like dominoes. The printed letters stood straight and even, much more legible but not as pretty.

Lydia sweetheart,
I was glad to hear you'd arrived safely and hadn't been kidnapped by a lonely millionaire who wanted

you to come and be his rich daughter. No such luck, right? We miss you. Daddy's feeling a little better. The treatment knocks him out, but he bounces back. Sometimes he feels strong enough to go for walks. He says the hospital's boring and all everyone does is watch the TV. Write to him, honey. It will cheer him up.

May mentioned day camp over the phone. I hope it's more fun than I remember.

It's terribly hot here. Yesterday I took four baths trying to stay cool. Take a swim in the lake for me. And climb to the top of the big pine next to the sunporch. Give May and Connie my love, and be a sweet, good girl like always. A million kisses plus one hundred butterfly kisses and one hundred Eskimo kisses,

Love,
Mom

Lydia loved to give butterfly kisses. You put your face up close and fluttered your eyelashes against someone's cheek. She tried one on the back of her hand. The light, nervous movement tickled.

It rained on Wednesday, so the campers couldn't go swimming or play outside. Instead a string of yellow school buses lined up at the curb.

"We're going to the Natural History Museum," announced the camp director. "Stay with your group, everyone. It's a big place and we don't want anyone to get lost. If you do, you might be history." She laughed at her own joke.

Lydia squeezed into a seat together with Emily and Ivy. As soon as the bus started to roll, a few campers began to sing. Soon everyone joined in, singing at the top of their lungs all the way to the museum. The songs were about bus wheels, sailors, peanuts and bottles of beer. Lydia picked up the words easily.

The buses lumbered through the rainy streets like a line of elephants holding tails, and finally parked in the museum driveway. Two large stone bears guarded the door to the museum.

"Stay together," reminded Miss Linda. She led them up the stairs. "We'll start with the animal exhibits, then visit the Indian rooms and the prehistoric wing."

Lydia followed the group down a dim hallway into the first room: Woodland Animals. Beavers paused by a half-finished dam, a fox and her cubs nestled in their den, deer stood amid ferns and trees, and a raccoon washed his food in a brook.

At first glance the dioramas looked lifelike. But Lydia noticed that the paint on the backgrounds was peeling and some of the animals' fur had fallen out in spots, like dogs with skin disease or teddy bears that had been loved bald.

They were all dead. Lydia shivered. She hoped they'd leave soon. This place made her sad. Even the guards looked faded and worn.

Miss Linda marched the Chickadees from room to room, never asking if they were tired or bored.

Leo and Johnny went by with their group, and called to Ivy and Emily. ''Wait until you see the Indians. Some are naked.'' Leo grinned.

''Yeah,'' said Johnny with a smirk. ''Titty, titty, titty.''

Finally it was time to go back to camp. The bus was hot and stuffy. None of the windows opened. The ride seemed twice as long as it had that morning.

First Lydia began to feel sweaty. Her head was hot and her eyes ached. Then the dizzy feeling came and her stomach swirled. Oh no, she thought. She was sitting on the very last seat between her friends, and she had to push her way to the front of the bus.

''Miss Linda, I'm going to throw up,'' she said.

''Can't you hold it?'' Miss Linda said.

Lydia shook her head.

After one look at Lydia's green face, Miss Linda tapped the driver on the shoulder. ''Sick kid,'' she said.

The driver scowled, but pulled over. Lydia managed to hold on until the doors opened. Then she leaned out and was very sick. Miss Linda made her sit right beside her the rest of the trip. Behind her, the other campers kept on singing while she huddled in the front seat, feeling green.

Back at camp, she walked around outside until she

felt better. Then she joined the group and even ate some of her lunch.

Ivy was missing. "Where is she?" Lydia asked Emily.

"Somebody took her lunch. She's trying to find it."

Ivy returned just then, scowling. "My mother put cookies in that lunch. Butterscotch chocolate chip. I'm going to find the thief. I am mad. Some creep's eating my cookies right this minute."

"Have the rest of my sandwich. I'm still not very hungry," Lydia said.

Ivy took a bite, then kept planning. "We've got to set a trap. Leo and Johnny will help."

"A trap?" Lydia asked.

"You know. Something that the thief will steal. A fake lunch."

"They put red dye on the money that they give to bank robbers. Then the red stuff gets all over them and everybody knows that they're the robbers," Emily said.

"That's an idea. But where can we get the dye?" Ivy asked.

Emily shrugged.

"We could use food coloring," Lydia suggested.

"Keep thinking of a plan. We'll have a meeting," said Ivy.

After lunch the whole camp watched cartoons on a movie screen in the front of the hall.

"Can you see?" Emily whispered.

"Not very well." Tiny figures raced frantically around the small screen.

"Let's play jacks in the corner," Emily suggested.

Talking in whispers, they played until the cartoons were over and it was time to go home.

"Is it always going to be like this?" Lydia asked Emily. "I'd have more fun staying home with my aunts."

"Don't stay home," said Emily. "We wouldn't get to play with you."

"We wouldn't be the three sillies," Ivy added.

So that night when Aunt May said, "How's camp?", Lydia answered, "It's okay."

But she told the truth in a letter to her father:

July 9

Dear Dad,

Camp stinks! It's the worst place I've ever been. At least I only have to go for one more week. I lost my underpants one day. Somebody stole my lunch. Then I got sick on the bus. They had to stop and wait while I threw up. I'd like to quit but I promised Emily and Ivy that I'd keep going. So don't tell anybody how bad it is, okay? I bet even the hospital's more fun than day camp! Hugs and kisses,

Lydia

STUCK IN THE
SHALLOW END

From the time Miss Linda first mentioned it, Lydia worried about the swimming test. She could see it in her mind. The campers would line up in bathing suits, all excited. One by one, they'd have to jump or dive into the water and swim across the deep end of the pool.

That wouldn't be any problem for most of the Chickadees. But Lydia had a secret that she'd hidden from her friends all week. She didn't know how to swim.

Swimming looked easy when someone else did it. At the pool, she watched the older kids playing tag in the deep end, diving under the surface or swimming quickly out of reach, churning the water with arms and legs.

She was glad her group had to stay in the shallow end this week.

"Let's play shark," Emily said.

Ivy, Lydia and three other Chickadees played. Ivy was it first. She swam underwater, stroking with one arm while the other stuck straight up like a fin. The girls jumped out of her way, half swimming, half walking in the waist-high water.

No one noticed that Lydia couldn't swim. She kept her feet on the bottom of the pool and managed to stay out of reach. She learned to take a breath of air, then dive underwater and stroke with her arms. When she needed air, she just stood up again.

"I'm cold," she told the others. "I'm going to sit in the sun for a while."

"But you haven't even been it yet," Ivy said.

"She's too fast for us," said Emily.

Lydia smiled and nodded, grateful to Emily for her answer.

She sat on the edge cross-legged, watching the game.

But what will I do on Monday? she wondered. I can't stand up in the middle of the deep end. And on one deep breath, I can only get to the middle of the pool.

A little later, she almost told Emily. They were lying on their towels by the side of the pool. Ivy was practicing swimming underwater, trying to get all the way to the other side on one breath.

"What happens if you don't pass the swimming test?" Lydia asked.

"It's not hard," said Emily. "Just one time across. Everybody passes."

"But what if someone didn't? What if they got halfway across and couldn't go any further?"

"I guess the lifeguard would jump in and rescue them."

Lydia glanced over at the lifeguard sitting on a tall white chair. A white safari hat shaded his eyes and a triangle of white sun block covered his nose. He sprawled on the chair with one arm leaning on the back. It was hard to imagine him moving quickly, even to rescue someone.

Emily's answer made Lydia feel worse. No one had ever failed the test. She'd be the first. She'd jump in, swim as far as she could underwater, then she'd run out of air and . . . and . . . and *sink!* Everyone would be watching. Someone would jump in and pull her out. She'd be so embarrassed. Or maybe they wouldn't even notice. She'd sink to the bottom and drown, without anyone ever knowing.

Lydia decided not to tell Emily her secret after all.

"All-camp assembly this afternoon," Miss Linda told them at lunch.

"Big deal," Ivy said when Miss Linda had gone

off to sit with the other counselors. She never ate with the group.

All the groups sat cross-legged facing the platform in the front of the hall. The director stood in front, wearing the same baseball cap and silver whistle. She looked more like an oversized kid than an adult.

"Campers, you're good sports, with spirit. We think you're the best group of campers we've ever seen." She paused, waiting for them to clap. Then she talked about team spirit and sportsmanship.

Lydia picked at the side of her sneaker while the director droned on. She managed to peel off a long piece of grayish rubber from around the heel. Finally the director read the name of the best camper from each group. "Let's give a big hand for each of these campers as they come up to get their Camper of the Week pins."

Monique won the Chickadee pin. She always stayed right by Miss Linda's side and did errands for her, running to the corner store to get her coffee in the morning and ice cream sandwiches after lunch.

"They should call it Slave of the Week," Ivy whispered as Monique went up front. Miss Linda heard her and glared. Ivy made a funny face when Miss Linda looked away again.

After the assembly, Lydia walked home with Emily and played some badminton. But even as she played, she kept thinking about swimming.

Lydia worried about the swimming test all day

Saturday. Maybe it will rain on Monday, she thought. Maybe the pool will crack in the middle and all the water will drain out. Maybe the lifeguard will get sick. Maybe I'll get sick, she thought.

Aunt Connie and Aunt May were concerned. They spoke gently and looked at her quizzically as if trying to guess the thoughts in her mind.

"Don't worry about your mother," Aunt May said as they were weeding the garden together. "She has everything under control."

Lydia nodded. She hadn't been thinking of her mother. She'd been trying to remember how many lanes there were in the pool.

"Lyddie, I am certain that your father is getting better. It doesn't do any good to fret on things," Aunt Connie said later as they chopped cucumbers and tomatoes for salad.

But Lydia hadn't been thinking of her father. She'd been wondering if it was possible to fake having the chicken pox.

Sunday was so hot that Lydia's nightgown was stuck to her back when she woke up. She pulled on her shortest shorts and a tank top and went downstairs in bare feet. Aunt May was puttering in the kitchen.

"Iced coffee, iced tea, cold orange juice, cold melon, and coffee cake—the coolest breakfast I can think of," she announced. "Served right now on the sunporch."

A slight breeze drifted through the porch screens.

Lydia read the comics while her aunts split the rest of the paper, trading sections as they finished them.

"Let's go to the quarry," Aunt May said, peering over the top of the paper. "Water's always cooler there."

"What's the quarry?" asked Lydia.

"It's a place where they cut huge blocks of rock out of the ground. After they took out all the rock, there was a deep hole and it filled with water from underground springs." Aunt May tried to describe it, but finally said, "Wait till you see it."

They drove out in the old green car. Lydia sat in the backseat with the picnic basket, army blanket, towels and books piled beside her. Aunt May's plain straw hat and Aunt Connie's flowered one blocked most of the windshield. Lydia looked out the side window.

To get to the quarry, they drove into the hills. Deep in the woods, Aunt May pulled off onto a dirt road and parked.

Lydia followed her aunts up a narrow path crowded by blueberry bushes. She couldn't see the quarry. Then the bushes stopped and she stepped out onto the rim. Rock ledges jutted out all around. In the center stood a deep pool of water with rocks, trees and sky mirrored in its still surface.

They spread the army blanket on a wide ledge overlooking the pool.

"I'm even hotter than I was before the car ride," said Aunt May.

Barefoot, she picked her way down the staircase of ledges until she reached the water's edge. Then in she dove, her bony white feet disappearing last, like pale fish sliding into the water. She broke the surface, shook her head and called, "Come in! It feels divine."

"May, you sound just like one of those travel ads on TV," Aunt Connie laughed. But she climbed down carefully and dove in without even a pause. In a few seconds she popped up right beside her sister.

"Your turn," she called to Lydia.

Lydia made her way down the rocks until she stood at the edge of the pool. Two shallow ledges lay just beneath the surface. Beyond them, the water stretched down and down, deeper than she could possibly see. Out in the middle her aunts floated calmly. The dark green water shimmered. Ripples from her aunts' strokes glinted in the sun.

Lydia shivered, and took a breath.

For an instant she thought she might just jump in. Step off the ledge and let the water fold around her. Sink down until she touched the bottom. Maybe she'd find another world. Maybe there was a castle there, dark green, made of emeralds.

Maybe she'd float instead. Or maybe she'd instantly know how to swim.

She looked once more at the deep pool. No, she

thought. Sometimes you just can't pretend. In a deliberately loud voice, big and firm to cover her embarrassment, she called to her aunts, "I can't swim."

"What's that, dear?" Aunt Connie cupped her hand to her ear.

"I can't swim."

Connie still looked confused but May explained. "She says she can't swim. It's too deep to wade."

Connie nodded, finally understanding.

"It's shallower over there at the far end," May called. "The ledges go out farther. You can wade in and cool off." She didn't sound upset by the news.

Lydia followed a path to the north end of the quarry. She waded out to her knees, then found a place where rocks made a chair. There she sat, with her head and shoulders above the water, letting her legs float.

After swimming for a while, her aunts climbed up to the blanket and lay in the sun. Lydia followed the path back and lay down beside them.

Aunt May, lying with her eyes closed, said gently, "Lydia, I didn't know you couldn't swim. Are they teaching you at camp?"

"No," said Lydia. "They don't know that I can't swim."

"They don't know? After one whole week?"

"The swim test is tomorrow. I won't pass. Emily and Ivy will. Then they'll go to the deep end and I'll be stuck with the little kids." Lydia's voice shook a little.

She didn't mention that she'd been pretending that she could swim and the others expected her to pass the test too.

May opened her eyes and peered over at her niece, shading her eyes. "Do you like camp?"

"Well," Lydia hesitated. "Actually . . . I *hate* it. All we do is sit around waiting to do the next thing. It's the most boring place I've ever been."

"My heavens, why didn't you tell us?" Aunt Connie said. She was sitting up now. "If you don't like it, you shouldn't go. Do the others like it?"

Lydia shook her head.

"As soon as we get home, I'm calling Emily's mother. I know we can come up with a better plan."

"Right," said Aunt May. "You can spend some time at home doing whatever you please. What's the summer for if you don't have time to just sit around or ride your bike?"

"Or sleep in the hammock," said Aunt Connie.

"Or go to the library," said Aunt May.

"Or play with the dollhouse," said Lydia, joining in with a giggle.

She eased her shoulders back onto the blanket and sighed. She could hardly believe it. She wouldn't have to take the test. She wouldn't have to go back to camp at all. No more sitting in circles. No more jolting bus rides or damp, smelly changing rooms. No more Miss Linda and her slaves.

She stared up at the sky, filled with relief. The sky

was deep enamel blue, the sun a pale silky yellow. She even heard a bird singing in the trees across the quarry. She felt so light, like a helium balloon. If she didn't hold on to the edge of the blanket, she might just sail away over the tops of the trees.

No more camp!

MAKING MONEY

Aunt Connie called Mrs. Mott and Mrs. Mott called Mrs. Ames. They decided that the girls would go to Pauling Lake for swimming and boating lessons every morning. In the afternoons they could entertain themselves.

"They'll be just fine," Lydia heard Aunt May saying over the phone. "Children have hundreds of ideas. And if they run out, we'll help them think of something. They can work on projects for the fair next month. It's judged by age, so they really do have a chance. Besides, it's more fun if you're in a contest."

Emily and Ivy were as happy as Lydia to stop going to camp. "I just wish we'd caught that kid who stole the lunches," Ivy said. "That's the only reason I wanted to go."

"Maybe Leo and Johnny will catch him," said Emily.

"Why do you think it's a boy?" asked Lydia. "It could be a girl."

"It could be anyone," mused Ivy.

"It could be Miss Linda," said Lydia, making Emily and Ivy shriek.

Lydia's swimming teacher, Ellen, was nothing like Miss Linda. She was tall and thin, so thin that her bones jutted out, ribs showing on her back, and hip-bones poking against the racing suit she wore. Ellen had short blonde hair and spoke in a soft voice.

"Don't be embarrassed about not knowing how to swim. I've taught people much older than you," Ellen said. "I've even taught grandmothers how to swim. Babies and grandmothers—the whole range."

Ellen taught her little by little how to breathe between strokes.

"It's a matter of rhythm," she explained. "When you're scared, you kick too hard and swing your arms like a waterwheel. Of course you can't take a breath. There isn't any time. You've got to slow down, relax and let the rhythm develop."

Lydia wanted to keep her head above the water, but Ellen wouldn't let her.

"The dog paddle's a baby stroke. You can't get any speed with it. Trust me. Put your face in the water and every time you lift your right arm, roll your face to the right and take a little gulp of air."

With Ellen's arms supporting her stomach, Lydia practiced stroking and breathing.

"That's it! Nice and easy," said Ellen.

Easy for you, you're standing up, Lydia thought as she moved her arms and kicked her legs.

"Relax. Pretend you're lying on your bed. The water will hold you if you relax."

Every morning after her swimming lesson, she practiced by herself until Emily and Ivy finished canoe class. To her surprise, in only a week she learned to stroke, kick and take a breath. When she got tired she rolled over on her back for a minute.

Ellen was surprised that Lydia could float on her back.

"My father taught me," Lydia told her.

He had cupped her head in his hand and let her body rise gently up until her legs floated to the top of the water. Gradually he'd convinced her that she wouldn't sink if she just eased her head back into the water and let her arms float. When she panicked, he'd rest her head against his shoulder and with one hand in the small of her back, keep her from sinking until she relaxed and became buoyant again.

"Mermaid" he called her because her hair floated on the water like a tangle of seaweed.

Before he could teach her any more, he got sick.

Lydia imagined what he would say if he could see her now. Sometimes she pretended that he was watching her practice.

In just a few weeks, if her father was stable, her mother would come for a short vacation.

A letter had come last week.

Dear Lydia,

Dad's improved so much that I think I'll be able to come up for a visit. The doctors are delighted. They say they've never seen someone respond so quickly. They keep bugging me to get a rest for myself. I guess I do need it. Yesterday I forgot that I left the water running in the tub upstairs, until water started dripping right onto the middle of the dining room table where I was having tea and reading. Hey, what're these spots on the newspaper? I said. Then I looked up and saw this mini-waterfall coming right out of the ceiling! Just call me Forgetful. What was my name, anyway? I'll try to get a flight the third week of August.

Can't wait to see you.

Love and hugs,
Mom

Lydia didn't think she could wait that long to see her. She'd bring her to the lake and show her how she could swim with her face in the water. Maybe by then she could swim all the way to the raft. They could swim out together.

At noon every day the girls went home for lunch. "Water rats," Aunt May teased, spreading towels for them on the backseat.

Sometimes they played together in the afternoon. Sometimes Lydia spent time by herself. Emily and Ivy worked on their fair projects but Lydia couldn't come up with any good ideas, so she played with the dollhouse, read books from the library and from the shelves in her bedroom—books her mother and her aunts had loved—and helped Aunt May in the garden. Sometimes she sorted file cards for Aunt Connie's book. The September deadline made Aunt Connie jumpy.

In sneakers and baggy shorts, Aunt May poked around each plant with a claw-shaped tool, pulling out tiny weeds before they had a chance to grow big.

"When you loosen the earth, it helps the plants. Loose soil holds the water better."

Aunt May's arms, legs and face were reddish brown and freckled. Around her eyes, tiny wrinkle lines were etched white against her tan.

"Lyddie, my love, did you ever hear of a monogrammed apple? You make one by putting tape on early. Then it ripens, leaving the taped part green."

With Aunt May's help, Lydia put an L on one apple, an E on another and an I on the third.

"We can be apple sisters," she told her aunt. "Like blood brothers."

"Easier than pricking your finger and mixing blood," Aunt May agreed.

When her aunt had moved on to the raspberry patch, Lydia chose another apple and taped M on it and C on the one beside it. The C needed six short pieces of tape to make it curved.

One day as the three girls waited for their ride home, Emily sprang a new idea on her friends. "I have a great plan, the best plan I've ever had." She was so excited that one word bumped into the next as they hurried to jump out. "We could start our own camp."

Lydia groaned. "Camp again?" She shivered just thinking of the Chickadees' circle and Miss Linda's braces gleaming in the sun. "What about our fair projects? I haven't even started."

Emily batted her objection away. "There's lots of time. I'm going to enter my tomatoes. They're doing better than anything else in the garden."

"I've got seven pot holders finished," Ivy said. "Double thickness."

"I don't know what to do," said Lydia.

"So think! You'll come up with something," said Emily. "But listen to my idea. We could start a playgroup for little kids, three- and four-year-olds. They'd come after their naps, say from two-thirty until four-thirty. We'll play games and make things. We'll make a lot of money."

"We could give them juice and cookies for snack. Animal crackers! Or Popsicles. The ice cream truck comes by every afternoon. I love snacks," Ivy said, already agreeing.

"There's three of us, and we're much bigger, so we won't have any trouble," Emily continued.

Lydia didn't say anything, but she had a feeling that Emily was wrong—they could have lots of trouble.

When they asked her, Mrs. Mott said the playgroup could meet in Emily's backyard. "The fence will help you keep track of the children. You can use the picnic table for snacks and arts and crafts."

Emily's swings had been given to a younger cousin, but her father dragged her old sandbox out of the back of the garage and filled it with clean sand.

Ivy's mother found a bunch of extra kitchen things for the sandbox: measuring cups, saucepans, old spoons, a sifter, and a stack of plastic containers.

Aunt Connie gave them a box of buttons. "Let them string these into necklaces," she said. Aunt May helped them make a flier describing the camp. Mr. Mott ran off copies at work.

"Now all we need is kids," Emily said, looking at the empty backyard.

"How can we find them?" asked Lydia, still half hoping that this plan would fall through.

"We'll take our fliers around and ask every mother we see," said Emily confidently.

"And we'll go to the houses of every kid we

already know," said Ivy. "Except Jimmy Smiley."

"He always cries when his mother won't buy him candy at the grocery store," Emily agreed.

Up and down the nearby streets, the girls rang doorbells, explained their plans and left fliers. They had four children signed up by the time they'd finished.

"We need more," said Ivy. "What about the apartment building? I bet there are kids living in there."

Lydia, who had no younger brothers or sisters, or even cousins, said, "Four's enough for me. There are only three of us, remember?"

"So what? We can each handle at least two or three of them. They're little," said Ivy. "Besides, the more kids we have, the more money we make."

Emily and Ivy decided to try ringing bells inside the apartment house while Lydia checked the park.

Under the maple tree next to the sandbox, a young woman in blue jeans sat on a bench, halfheartedly watching twin boys pour buckets of sand over each other's head.

"Tim's taking a shower," said one.

"Joey's taking a shower too," said the other.

"Your hair's all wet with sand."

"Not as wet as yours."

They teased each other into pouring more and more sand until they were throwing handfuls with both fists.

Dodging the flying grains, Lydia smiled shyly and handed the woman a flier.

"My friends and I are running an afternoon play-group for little kids. We'll have games, snacks and things to make. There's a grown-up helping us, my friend's mother. It starts next week."

"How long will you keep them?" the woman said.

"From two-thirty until four-thirty."

"It's better than nothing. Will you take these two?"

"Sure. Just fill in the application."

As the woman was writing her name and address at the bottom of the flier, Lydia spied her friends and waved.

"It starts Monday at this address. You can call Mrs. Mott if you have any questions." She tore off the top half of the flier and gave it to the woman. With a last glance at Tim and Joey, she ran to catch up with Ivy and Emily.

"I got two. They're twins."

"Good. We got three more. That's nine in all. Three each," said Emily. "We'll be rich enough to buy anything we like by the time the summer's over. I want a tape recorder."

"I want a new bike," said Ivy.

"We won't make that much," said Lydia.

"We will too, if the playgroup lasts all summer," Ivy insisted. "That's about six more weeks, or at least five more."

Lydia didn't answer. Nine little kids for the rest of the summer!

"Nine little children sounds like a lot to me," said Aunt May when Lydia returned home. "They'll keep you hopping."

"Three each," said Lydia.

"You've only got hands for two. You'll have to sit on the third, I guess."

"May, don't get her worried. What could go wrong in Emily's backyard?" Aunt Connie said.

Aunt May smiled. "Plenty," she predicted.

On the first day the children arrived in ones and twos. Some skipped up the driveway, waved goodbye to their mothers and began to explore the sandbox. Others hugged their mothers' arms like small boa constrictors and had to be pried loose.

Finally five little girls and four little boys gathered in the yard.

"Okay, everybody, let's sit in a circle," Emily said. She and Ivy and Lydia got the children seated. Lydia gave out name cards. At Mrs. Mott's suggestion, Emily had written each child's name on a heavy cardboard circle and strung each on a piece of yarn.

"Put your name around your neck," Ivy told them.

Once they were labeled, the children played Duck, Duck Goose, Ring-around-the-rosy, A-tisket a-tasket and London Bridge. They giggled and squealed.

"They really like this stuff," Lydia said to Ivy in surprise. "I hate circle games."

"You're not three years old," Ivy said.

But the games didn't keep them happy for long. Soon Tim and Joey, the red-haired twins, drifted

away and began to wrestle. They were quickly joined by Harry, Michael and a girl named Roberta. Michael cried when Roberta pulled his hair.

"Stupid baby," she called him, making him cry even harder.

"Who wants to make something with Play-Doh?" Emily asked, luring everyone to the picnic table. For a few calm minutes all nine were busy thumping, rolling, cutting and prodding the squishy stuff that the girls had prepared that morning.

"What time is it?" Ivy asked.

Lydia checked her watch. "Only three o'clock."

"This is harder than I thought," Ivy said.

"He put Play-Doh in my hair," whined Louise, pointing at Harry.

"I did not. I made a bug and it jumped." Blue streaks decorated Harry's face like Indian war paint.

Then they had snack—apple juice and graham crackers. While the others sat quietly eating, Tim and Joey discovered the garden hose and made a puddle. By the time the girls noticed, Tim was sitting happily in the center of the puddle stirring the muddy water with both hands. Joey still manned the hose, spreading the puddle into Mrs. Mott's rose garden.

"Mud pies!" said Isabelle.

It was impossible to keep the other children away from the giant puddle. Finally the girls gave up and let them play in it.

"But take off your shoes," Emily said.

For the rest of the afternoon, eight children mixed mud pies, sailed leaf boats and waded in circles around Tim, who refused to move from the center of the puddle.

"I'm a hippo," he explained. "This is my house."

"You're all wet. Your mother will be mad," Lydia said. She was worried because she'd signed him up.

"Don't care," said Tim.

"You'll have to take a bath," said Lydia.

"Don't care," Tim repeated.

Lydia shrugged and sat down beside her friends. The children mucked in the puddle, happy as piglets.

"Just before playgroup ends, we'll hose down their arms and legs, dry them off and they'll be okay. They're having fun," said Ivy.

"More fun than we had in camp," Lydia agreed.

When it was four-fifteen, Ivy sprayed the mud off everyone's arms and legs. Emily and Lydia dried them and helped put on sandals and sneakers. They even wiped the mud off their faces. Only Tim looked as though he had taken a mud bath. The girls tried to wipe him clean, but his clothes stayed grimy and damp.

His mother didn't say a word about it.

"Maybe he always looks like that by the end of the day," said Lydia.

"Maybe she's so glad to get rid of him for a while that she doesn't care what he looks like," said Emily.

It rained on Tuesday, so playgroup was canceled.

On Wednesday they decided to go on a trip.

"We have to," said Lydia. "They've already wrecked the yard."

"Let's take them to the rocks down by the railroad station," said Ivy.

"Those are too high. Little kids can't climb that high," said Emily.

"Sure they can. I always did. I climbed them when I was a baby," Ivy answered.

Lydia imagined Ivy in her diapers crawling up the side of a huge rock.

"Okay, we'll give it a try," said Emily.

It took almost half an hour to walk nine little kids two blocks to the park near the station.

First Isabelle stopped to pet a large gray cat sleeping peacefully on the hood of a car. Then the others all wanted to pet him too.

Then Harry had to go to the bathroom and he wouldn't just go in the bushes as Ivy suggested. So they went back to the Motts' house and everyone took a turn.

When they finally reached the park, the girls were as hot and grumpy as the small campers.

Ivy pointed to the highest spot, a flat surface on top of the biggest boulder. "First one to the top wins the race."

Tim and Joey needed no encouragement. They climbed like monkeys, finding footholds easily, and ignoring any scrapes. Roberta climbed almost as fast but her sandals slipped more than sneakers. The two slowest were Harry and Angela. Harry was afraid of falling. Angela had trouble balancing. But little by little, they inched up the rocks until they, too, sat cross-legged in the sun eating raisins and peanuts.

"This is mountain climbers' food," Emily told them. "It's called gorp."

"I'm thirsty," said Joey. "Can I have a drink?"

"There's nothing to drink," said Emily.

"If we got stuck up here, we'd need water," said Harry. "Ranger Rick says hikers need water." Harry was almost five, and knew more than the other kids.

The children looked at each other. Their mouths made little Os and their eyes were round.

"We're not getting stuck," Ivy said, but the campers weren't convinced.

"I want my mother," Isabelle whined.

"Me too," said Louise in a teary voice.

Mary began to cry loudly. "We're stuck. I want to go home. Mommy! I want my mommy! Mom-my!" Her voice sailed out into the air like a siren.

"Wait a minute, you guys." Ivy tried to reason with them. "Didn't I just say we are *not* stuck? We'll just climb down right now and you'll see how simple it is. You crybabies are ruining all the fun."

To prove her point, Ivy stood up. "Who's ready?" she asked, and began to climb down the hill. Tim and Joey followed right behind her. Then Roberta half climbed, half slid down a smooth, steep side. Holding hands, Mary and Louise inched down on their stomachs.

"I'll take Harry and Michael. You take Angela and Isabelle," Emily told Lydia. "Come on, guys. Pretend you're being chased by a bear." She left with the boys happily screaming, "Help! He's right behind us."

Angela and Isabelle were both sniffling. Isabelle needed a handkerchief badly. Lydia found a tissue in her pocket and helped her swab her nose.

"Looks like we'll be the last ones," she said.

"I'm scared," said Angela. "I'll fall off."

"No you won't," said Lydia.

Isabelle decided to try going down by herself. "Last one down's a rotten egg," she said, inching her way off the top of the rock.

As Isabelle disappeared, Angela began to cry again.

"Don't cry," Lydia said. "So what if we're last?"

Angela looked down at the train station across the street. "My daddy takes the train to the city. Maybe he'll come home soon and get me down." She began to cry harder. "I wish my daddy was here right now."

Angela's face was pink with red blotches on her cheeks and forehead. Her eyes and mouth were twisted and scrunched from crying, and her nose was running thickly onto her upper lip. She looked like a combination of a giant newborn baby and an ugly old troll. For a moment, Lydia wished she could just leave her behind.

"I want my daddy," Angela moaned.

Me too, thought Lydia. My dad would know what to do. Even the dollhouse father had known what to do.

The two girls sat for a few minutes, Angela sniffling, Lydia thinking of her father. Suddenly she felt like crying too. She reached over and gave the little girl a hug. "We don't need your father to get us down. How about this? We can make a train and slide down together. I'll sit in front and you hold on to my middle."

We better not fall or I'll get squished, she thought. This kid probably weighs about a hundred pounds.

Angela's face brightened. "Let's pretend we're the little engine that could."

Lydia nodded and sat down. Angela sat behind her, round legs sticking out on either side and arms clenched around Lydia's stomach.

"Not so tight," Lydia gasped.

"I think I can. I think I can," Angela chanted.

Lydia gripped the rock with her hands and the soles of her sneakers. Little by little, they slid down the first rock.

"I think I can. I think I can," Angela crowed happily.

The next rock wasn't so smooth. Sliding wouldn't work.

"Pretend that this is a ladder and you're a fire-man," said Lydia.

Angela didn't want to. "You can be the fireman and I'll be the baby. You carry me down."

"Carry you? Are you crazy?" Lydia couldn't even imagine lifting her off the ground one inch. "No. We're both firemen."

She started to climb down the rock step by step.

Angela didn't move.

"Come on!" Lydia said.

Angela sat down right where she was and didn't budge.

"It's easy," Lydia coaxed. "Just put your feet on the little ledges and step down."

"I'll slip." Angela's lower lip stuck out like a fat worm.

"No you won't."

"Yes I will."

"Then I'll catch you." And we'll both fall, Lydia thought to herself. "If you climb down, I'll give you a piece of bubble gum."

Angela finally started to move, stepping down the rock with surprising grace.

Lydia didn't pause until they landed on the grass. The others were lying in the shade, waiting.

"What took you so long?" Ivy asked.

Lydia frowned and shook her head. What good was it to try to explain?

"We were playing train," said Angela, her face

gleaming. "Where's my gum?" she asked Lydia.

Lydia fished her last piece out of her pocket.

"If playgroup lasts any longer than Friday, I quit," she said to Ivy and Emily.

From the tone of her voice, they both knew she wasn't kidding.

That night she described the rock-climbing escapade in a letter to her father:

Dear Dad,

The playgroup for little kids is a big mistake. Nine kids make a lot of trouble! We took them to climb some rocks today, and I got stuck at the top of the hill with a blubbering three-year-old. It took forever to get her down. Afterward, I told Emily and Ivy that I didn't want to do the playgroup anymore. They want to run it all summer, so we'd make a lot of money. But Mrs. Mott says we'd better stop before anyone gets hurt. I'm glad! I still have to think up a project for the fair next month. Do you have any ideas? I'm glad you're feeling well. Mom said you walked for a whole hour last week. That's great!

I love you,
Lydia

PUZZLES

Ivy was disappointed that the playgroup was ending. "I had my bike all picked out."

"Maybe your parents will lend you the rest," said Lydia.

"I've got about half what I need for the tape recorder," said Emily. "I'm going to keep on saving. Or maybe I'll get it for Christmas."

"At least we made *some* money," said Lydia.

"Not enough." Ivy refused to be cheered up.

"It's a lot to me," said Lydia. "Maybe I'll buy a tape for my father. And I'll buy some books, and a new sweatshirt, and maybe a musical jewelry box, and something for my aunts."

"You don't have that much money," said Emily.

"Well, I can get some of them," Lydia said.

"Maybe I'll get a sweatshirt too," said Emily.

"We could all get ones that matched," said Ivy, finally perking up. "And we could get a croquet set to share."

"Or a microscope," said Emily. "I always wanted one of those. We could collect water from the pond and see all the little creatures."

"Or a telescope! We could put the money together and get one of those," said Ivy.

"I always wanted an ant farm," said Lydia. "You can watch the ants make little roads and you can see inside their houses."

"I always wanted one of those too," said Ivy.

"Let's each get an ant farm and a sweatshirt," said Emily.

On Friday, when the last sticky child had been claimed by a parent, Lydia said goodbye to Emily and Ivy and headed home, tired and relieved. "If I don't see another little kid all year, I'll be happy," she said.

That night Aunt Connie made a blueberry pie to celebrate.

"No casualties," she explained. "And the three of you are still friends."

That morning Aunt May had found three old jig-saw puzzles at a yard sale. "Let's try one after dessert."

The boxes had no pictures to give them clues, so Lydia picked one by saying eenie, meenie, miney, moe.

Aunt May dumped the pieces out on the dining room table. "We turn them all over first," she said. "I like the border. You can work on any part you like."

The puzzle had lots of blue for the sky. Or maybe for water, Lydia thought. And dark red that could be brick houses or a barn. Brown and green and very bright yellow. Lots of gray and white.

"Let's all guess what it is," said Aunt Connie.

They studied the pieces.

"I say it's a farm," said Aunt May.

"I say it's Paris in the fall," said Aunt Connie.

Lydia kept on looking. What would have those colors? "A castle with a moat," she guessed.

They got to work. May pieced the border. Connie started on the dark red and Lydia collected all the gray. It looked like parts of a stone wall. They each worked quietly for a while, sending the right kind of pieces over to each other. Connie hummed and tapped her foot against her chair.

"Now that the playgroup is over, I bet it won't be long before Emily comes up with a new plan," said Aunt Connie. "I wonder where she gets those schemes."

Lydia shrugged. "From her brain, I guess."

"She's always been like that," Aunt Connie continued. "Ever since she was a little thing. Full of ideas."

"Emily's the brains but Ivy's the wit," said Aunt May.

"What's wit?" asked Lydia.

"Being funny, clever, full of jokes."

That sounded like Ivy, Lydia thought. Emily was smart and Ivy was funny. And Lydia was ... ? She didn't have a word to finish the sentence. I'm not dumb but I'm not so smart. I like to have fun but I'm not so funny. What am I?

Asking felt awkward. It was like saying "Am I pretty?" or "Do you like me?" but Lydia needed to know.

"What do you think I am?"

Both her aunts looked up from the puzzle, surprised. Aunt May looked like the wise old owl peering over her round glasses. She needed glasses for reading and for puzzles too.

"What do you mean?" she asked.

Lydia blushed. She wasn't exactly sure what she meant. But she tried to explain herself.

"Emily's smart, right? Ivy's funny. Leo's a clown. Johnny's wild. But what am I? I'm not anything."

Aunt May chuckled. "You want a label, that's what you're asking for." She shook her head. "Labels don't fit everyone. Maybe they don't fit anyone."

"Why not?"

"We just aren't one way or one thing. We're lots

of things, all at the same time. I never had a label. But Connie did, didn't you?''

Aunt Connie groaned. "I hated it."

"Tell me, please?"

"I was a chicken. Too scared to try anything. I wouldn't climb trees. I wouldn't even go sliding on the pond with the others. They teased me all the time."

"But you grew out of it," May defended her.

"You *did* have a label, May," Connie said. "You were the bookworm."

May laughed. "I forgot that. Yes, that's what Father always called me."

"There were even special family rules for May," Aunt Connie told Lydia. "No reading until your homework is finished."

"Remember this one? No spinach, no books?" May said.

"See!" said Lydia. "Everyone has a label except me. I don't do anything special. I'm not anything special."

Both aunts looked over at her again, this time more carefully. They heard the hurt in her voice.

"Your looks are special," Aunt Connie said. "Those braids and big gray eyes make you look old-fashioned, like a girl in a fairy tale. Someone that special things might happen to. Not just ordinary. Imaginative, dreamy."

May nodded in agreement. "Yes, there is that other-time quality. You're strong too. Independent. I think it comes from being on your own so much since your father's been sick. You take your time, and you find your own way.''

The list kept growing as the aunts added to it.

''You're kind, Lyddie. When you think about your mom and your dad, or worry about the little kids at playgroup, you put yourself in their place,'' said Connie. ''You've got a good heart, as they say.''

May shook her head. ''I still say you don't need a label. They don't fit people anyway. Maybe sometimes Leo's a clown, but not all the time. And Johnny just got stuck with that reputation. Labels box you in. It's much better not to have one.''

Lydia pushed over three border pieces she'd found.

''I still wish I was one thing special.''

''Some people find their special things later. You're more mysterious this way, sweetheart. Like a secret country that hasn't been fully explored,'' said Aunt May, snapping a corner piece into place.

''Like the puzzle,'' Aunt Connie said, pleased with herself for thinking up the comparison. ''We aren't sure what it's going to be yet. There's some of this and some of that in it. We have to wait and see how it turns out.''

''How about some popcorn while we're waiting?'' asked Aunt May.

''Yes, please,'' said Lydia. ''And some ginger ale.''

Mysterious, that's what I am, she thought with a

satisfied smile. She fit another piece of gray onto the wall. I was right, this is going to be a castle. I win.

With the little kids' playgroup over, Lydia had afternoons to herself again. She tried to think up a project for the fair. It was already the first week in August and she still didn't have an idea.

"Enter some vegetables," Aunt May suggested. "You've been helping with the weeding and watering."

"But I didn't plant them, so they're not really mine."

"You could plant something that comes up fast, like radishes."

Lydia imagined herself standing in front of a panel of judges holding a bunch of radishes. She'd feel ridiculous. Radishes were so small. People just cut them into little flowers and stuck them on the side of a plate. Besides, they didn't even taste very good.

"I want my own project but I can't think of anything to make. I hate to sew. I can't cook anything except toast."

"You could learn. Any fool can cook. Not that I think you're a fool, dear, but it's much easier than you think. Connie's the one to ask. She's a much better cook than I am."

"Maybe I'll ask her," Lydia said.

The next weekend Aunt Connie invited the Motts and the Ameses over for a barbecue. Everyone sat in the grassy backyard and ate ribs dripping with hot sauce, corn on the cob, salad picked fresh from the garden, and rolls that Connie had baked that afternoon. Fingers were sticky, faces were smeared with sauce. Even the pesky mosquitoes kept away for once.

After dinner they split and sliced a big watermelon. "How about a seed-spitting contest?" suggested Mr. Mott. "Everyone line up on the edge of the walk."

Lydia stood between Ivy and Aunt Connie. Watermelon juice dripped down her chin.

"With this gap in my teeth, I've got a natural advantage over the rest of you," Aunt Connie teased.

At first everyone aimed out at the lawn and tried to spit their seeds the farthest. Then they aimed at each other, and the contest became a watermelon war.

"Enough, enough," laughed Mr. Mott when Emily's seed slid down his neck. "Why don't you girls play tag or something?"

He sat down on a lawn chair to rest. Emily immediately sat on his knees, still bouncing a little from the excitement of the game. He tickled the back of her neck with a blade of grass. Watching them, Lydia wished that her father could be there too.

"Come on, small fry, leave us in peace for a while," Mr. Mott urged, nudging Emily off his lap.

The girls wandered toward the front yard. Three wasn't enough for tag, so they drew hopscotch snails in chalk on the street and played until it was too dark to see the squares.

"Let's play Ring-a-levio tomorrow night," said Ivy. "See how dark it is? It's perfect for hiding. Meet at my house. I'll tell everybody, okay?"

The next night, after dinner, Emily knocked on the kitchen door. Lydia was loading the dishwasher.

"Bring a dark sweatshirt. It helps when you're hiding. Those shorts are good." Emily pointed to Lydia's navy hiking shorts. Emily was dressed in dark green.

When they reached Ivy's house, Leo and Johnny Ringer sat on the porch steps with Phyllis, who lived at the end of the street. Phyllis's little sister, Amy, stood awkwardly on the grass beside the steps, hoping they would let her play. Two girls from the Chickadees sat next to each other on the porch swing. They both had red hair, freckles and names that began with M, Mary and Margaret. Their grandmother lived across the street from Ivy, and ever since camp, they came over a lot.

"Oh good, we can start," Ivy said when she saw Emily and Lydia. "Leo's captain and so am I. Come on, Leo, let's shoot."

"Odds," Leo called. Ivy nodded.

One, two, three, *shoot!* Two fingers each, an even pair. Ivy's.

One, two, three, *shoot!* A one and a two. Odds. Leo's.

One, two, three, *shoot!* One finger each. Even. Ivy's.

One, two, three, *shoot!* Two each again. A pair.

"I win," Ivy said. "I pick Johnny."

"Emily," said Leo. "I need some smarts on this team."

Ivy said, "Lydia, over here."

The others were picked one by one. Ivy's team had five, Leo's had four. But the larger team had Amy, who couldn't run as fast.

Since Ivy had first choice, Leo's team was first to hide.

"No peeking," Emily said.

Ivy's team all covered their eyes and leaned against the trees, counting out loud as fast as they could while the other team ran off. Ivy kept counting until she reached two hundred. "Ready or not, here we come," she called. "Okay," she said to the others, "spread out and get ready to tag. Be listening for the call. If you hear it, run for base. If you get there before the other team, you can tag them there."

Lydia began to look by the garden where the bushes grew along the side of the fence. The shadows were dark, but she could see faintly into the corners and the bushes. She shivered. Anything might be hiding in the darkness. Maybe snakes.

Why didn't I stay with Ivy, she thought. She said to spread out. I could've stayed with Amy though, and pretended to keep her company.

She circled back toward base. Squares of light from the kitchen windows glowed on the grass. Safety zone,

Lydia thought, stepping deliberately into a bright square.

"Watch out," someone whispered. "They'll see you."

Lydia recognized Johnny's voice.

"Who'll see me?"

"Leo's team. Stay in the shadows. You have to surprise them or they can race you to base." He was standing behind the fir tree at the corner of the house. Lydia joined him.

"I checked under the porch and behind the garage," he whispered. "I bet they're up in some tree or across the street. Come on. Let's check behind the stone wall."

"But Ivy said spread out," Lydia whispered.

"So? There's no rules about looking together. It's more fun. If we find them, we can tag more."

Delighted to have an excuse not to be alone, Lydia followed. They tiptoed down the edge of the driveway, staying off the telltale gravel with its noisy crunch. When they reached the sidewalk, Johnny began to run. Lydia tried to keep up. She wasn't sure what stone wall he was talking about. When the game was described, she imagined it all happening inside Ivy's yard. But now she realized that it extended out into the whole neighborhood.

Johnny paused at a driveway and waited for a minute with a finger on his lips, listening.

"Come on, the wall's over here," he whispered,

starting across the street but staying out of the bright circle cast by the streetlight. "I'll check that end, you check the other. Either way they run, we'll get them."

Johnny climbed over the wall and dropped into the dark shadow on the other side.

Lydia hesitated for a moment. It was inky dark below. Snakes could lie coiled in the grass. Hungry snakes. Boas and rattlers, just waiting for a juicy kid to eat for a snack. But Johnny had jumped and she didn't want him to think she was afraid.

Thud. She landed on the springy grass. She inched forward in the inky darkness, trying hard to see in front of her.

Suddenly her foot struck something bulky and she fell forward.

"Oof! Watch it!" Leo grunted.

"Here they are!" Lydia screamed.

"Run," Leo yelled to his team.

"Tag them," Johnny said.

She tried, touching Leo and someone else's arm. The others ran but Johnny cut them off.

"Tag one, tag two," he yelled.

"I got two," said Lydia.

"Ring-a-levio!" Johnny yelled. "Nice try," he said to Leo, who was still sitting on the ground where Lydia had pinned him.

Both teams gathered back at the tree. "Who found them?" Ivy asked.

"Lydia," said Johnny, giving her a thump on the back.

"But Johnny knew where to look," Lydia said.

"Go hide," Leo said. "We'll start counting."

Ivy led them down the driveway. Johnny and Ivy deliberately crunched the gravel. At the side of the road they paused.

"Sssh," whispered Ivy. "We're going back to the garage. Walk on the grass and don't make a sound."

Single file, they tiptoed.

"The roof?" Johnny whispered.

"Climb on the woodbox first, then the gas tank. It's easy from there," Ivy said.

She was up in seconds. Lydia followed, trying not to bump her feet. Margaret needed a hand up and Amy had to be pulled. She scraped her knee on the shingles. Lydia knew it must hurt, but Amy didn't cry. Last of all, Johnny swung up as smoothly as if he were pulled by wires. They lay on their stomachs, peering out at the backyard.

"They went down the driveway." Emily's voice carried from the front of the house.

Ivy giggled, delighted to have fooled them.

"Sssh," Johnny cautioned. "As soon as they turn the corner, we sneak down and head back around the other side of the house. Then we run for it." His whisper was so low that Lydia heard only every other word, and had to fill in the blanks herself.

They waited until the last crunch of gravel faded.

"Now!" Johnny whispered.

He dropped down easily. Ivy slid backward on her belly until her feet touched the gas tank. Then she jumped to the ground.

"I can't get down," whispered Margaret in a teary voice.

"My knee hurts," Amy said.

Lydia was anxious to be off toward base.

"Just slide down until you touch the tank," she said. "Ivy did it."

Margaret said, "I can't."

Amy sniffed.

"Move over and watch me," Lydia said, sliding easily down. "Come on. If I can do it, so can you. Hurry or we'll get caught."

Finally the others managed. Once on the ground, they headed across the backyard and up along the side of the house. Ivy checked the front yard to see if it was safe.

"Go as fast as you can. They've got to tag three. Ready?"

Feeling fast and sneaky as a spy, Lydia ran for the tree, not stopping until she touched its crinkled bark.

"Ring-a-levio!"

The other team straggled back in ones and twos.

"We thought you'd gone out the driveway," Emily said. "Where were you?"

Ivy grinned. "Secret."

"Come on," said Leo.

Ivy shook her head. "Two to nothing. First to get three wins the game," she reminded him.

"Make it four," he said.

"Three," she repeated. "We can't stay out any later."

"You won't get this point," he said. "Come on, team."

Lydia covered her eyes and began to count. When they reached two hundred, they scattered again. Lydia met Johnny by the mailbox.

"Stick with me," he whispered. "Maybe we'll get lucky again."

She did, happily. They checked inside the cellar door at the top of the steps, under the porch, inside the extra garbage cans, under the car.

"My dad's car is just like this," Lydia said.

"Nice car," he said.

"There's no one to drive it now," Lydia said. Then, realizing that Johnny might not know, she said, "My dad's in the hospital."

"Ivy told me. Do you miss him?"

Lydia shrugged. "Sometimes." Being in the darkness together made it easy to talk even though she didn't know Johnny well at all.

"Let's try the garage next door," he said after a moment.

They squeezed through a missing slat in the fence. The garage was empty.

Walking back, Johnny blurted out, "My dad's gone."

"Oh?" Lydia didn't know what he meant. "Did he die?"

"No, he went away when I was still a baby."

"Where'd he go?"

"I don't know. I don't remember him. My mom showed me his picture in their high school yearbook. She says I look like him."

Lydia was amazed. She had a million questions but she was afraid to ask any. Where did his father go? Why? Why would a father leave his baby? How could Johnny say it so plainly? Wasn't he sad?

"It's not so bad," Johnny said with a shrug. "My uncle comes to Scouts with me when I need him. He coaches my baseball team too. Most of the time, it's okay."

He seemed eager to reassure her, but Lydia still couldn't believe any father would just disappear. Why didn't the police catch him and make him come back?

"Ring-a-levio!" The shout was over on the other side of base.

"Let's go. I wonder where they tagged them," Johnny said, starting to run.

The game ended 3–0. Leo tried to be a good sport about it even though he wanted one more try.

"I promised I'd be inside by nine," Ivy apologized.

Walking back with Emily, Lydia thought about Johnny. She wished she could talk to Emily about it, but she didn't want to tell a secret, if it was a secret.

Maybe she could ask her aunts in the morning. They'd be careful not to tell anyone. How could someone just leave? She wanted an answer.

The next morning, weeding again with Aunt May, Lydia asked, "Why would someone go away and leave their child?"

Aunt May sat back on her heels and pushed up her straw hat so she could look directly at her niece. "Now what on earth put that thought in your head?"

"Promise not to tell anyone? I think it's a secret."

After hearing the story, Aunt May shook her head. "It's not a secret, Lyddie, not in a town this size. We all knew what happened. Steven Ringer didn't leave Johnny, really. He left the whole idea of marriage, family, job. He hadn't grown up yet himself. As I remember, he headed for Alaska in hopes of working on the pipeline. Some people take a long time to grow up, sweetheart, and that's hard on their children."

"But it's not fair. Johnny didn't do anything."

"You're right, it isn't fair. Johnny would love to have a father, I'm sure. Maybe he'll get one. His mother might marry again."

"He told me it wasn't so bad not having a father, but I think he was just trying to make me feel better," Lydia said. "In case Dad doesn't get well."

"I always liked that boy," Aunt May said. "Even

when he wrote WITCH on the door with shaving cream one Halloween. But I do think Mike is getting better, Lyddie. That's what the doctors say."

Lydia went back to weeding, scraping at the tough little vines with the claw tool. For the first time she tried to imagine what it would be like not to have a father. Not just one who was away or sick a lot. None. No one. Just a gap beside her mother and herself.

Lydia thought of her dad, tall and thin, walking with a little bounce as if he had a private song playing in his head, laughing a little and squeezing her hand lightly.

She hoped Aunt May was right. He had to get better.

That afternoon she walked to the drugstore and picked out a trick postcard to send him. A farmer stood beside a tomato as big as himself, and underneath it said, "We grow 'em big." How do they make it look like that? she wondered as she thought of what to write.

Hi, Dad,
I bet this man wins a prize at the fair. We had a barbecue on Sunday, and last night we played ring-a-levio in the dark. I miss you.

The card didn't have room for more. She signed it "Love and kisses, Lydia," and mailed it on her way home.

MAGIC BOXES

The next week it rained every day. The garden grew high and the leaves turned deep green. Everyone's tans faded, turning slightly yellow. Swimming lessons were canceled. And Emily didn't want to play.

"I've got to read for the library summer reading contest. I won't get to go to the ice cream party if I don't get some more books finished."

"Why do you care about the contest, anyway? What's so great about moving a marker across a map?" Lydia asked.

This year the markers were covered wagons made from cardboard and construction paper. Emily had drawn a girl in a bonnet sitting on the seat of hers. "I'm halfway across the prairie. Some people have reached the mountains already. Why didn't you enter?"

"I don't like contests. I just like to read."

Lydia agreed to go the library with Emily, though, and help her pick out more books. They each brought home four.

Emily settled down on her living room couch, and soon all Lydia could hear was the sound of a page turning every few minutes. She sat in a big wing chair, with her head resting on the side and her legs slung over the arm. In her book, a talking pig had escaped and had to be found. The pig keeper was out searching. Even though it had an exciting beginning, Lydia began to feel restless. She liked to read at night best, lying in bed. Emily looked so comfortable and involved, Lydia didn't disturb her.

"See you later," she said, and let herself out the front door.

It was raining too hard to go for a walk or work in the garden. She stepped in every puddle between Emily's house and hers. Her sneakers squished and slurped.

She found Aunt May on the sunporch reading.

"Where's Aunt Connie?" Lydia asked.

"Gone shopping. She tried to find you."

"I went to the library with Emily."

"She couldn't wait. She'll be back about five."

Lydia left the room and climbed the stairs slowly, letting each foot drag on the edge of the step. What would she do? If she'd gone with Aunt Connie, they could've had ice cream sodas at Jimmy's, where the seats turned all the way around and you could spin yourself while you waited.

Aunt Connie always let her buy what she wanted, provided she had her own money to spend, even if it was something silly, like a little ballerina statue or a pencil with a gumball machine on the end instead of an eraser. If she bought one of those, she could put the gumball machine in the dollhouse when she'd used up the pencil.

Maybe she'd work on the dollhouse today. She still needed to think up a project for the fair too.

The rain was coming down hard now, streaming over the window. Lydia turned on the light next to her bed and examined the dollhouse. The family looked just as bored as she felt. Everyone just sat. Even the cook.

"What's wrong with you guys? Come on, we have to get going here. Cooky, let's make brownies."

She put the cook in front of the table and set out a bowl and a pan.

"Kids, don't you want to help? Get down here and bother Cook."

Soon everyone was busy. Cook and the children clustered in the kitchen, Mother was at the piano, Father was at his desk and the baby was chasing the cat around the living room rug.

Once she'd put everyone in place, Lydia couldn't think of anything else to do.

I could make new furniture, she thought. But it's more fun with Emily. She has good ideas, like using sponges for chairs, and more stuff. I only have scissors, cardboard and glue.

She wandered around her room, picking up odds and ends lying on the shelves or the top of the dresser, shells and sea glass from the beach, a blue feather, two tiny bears holding hands.

For a while she stared at the window, making believe there were races between the raindrops. Picking two that were starting at the same time, she'd bet on one, then follow them as they rolled down the glass. Sometimes a drop hit another drop, and got stuck. But sometimes, if it hit another and got bigger, it would move faster and faster.

When that grew dull, she sat down in the rocker and rocked back and forth, looking around the room, hoping for a new idea.

An envelope lay on her bedside table, with her father's handwriting on it. When it came in the mail yesterday, she'd read it quickly. She opened it again now.

Sweetheart, how are you? I hope you're having fun. I think of you playing and swimming and it cheers me up. Sounds like you're making progress with the swimming. I'd love to see you. Remember when we used to go to the pond together?

I'm feeling pretty good. The treatments are work-ing, the doctor says. I can't tell, myself. I look funny bald, like that character on Bugs Bunny. Elmer Fudd, that's what you can call me. Send me a letter soon. I get so bored. I wouldn't even mind if that pesky rabbit came along and bothered me. I hope I'll be home by the end of the summer.

Love, kisses and a big squeeze from your Dad

It sounded just like him, joking about his bald head. Lydia knew that was from the treatment and the medication. Poor Dad. He was bored, just like her. If he was here, they could play cards. Hey, maybe she'd make him a card to cheer him up. Then she could walk down to the post office and mail it.

She started to collect everything she needed: paper, crayons, markers, scissors and glue, and some stickers.

Right next to the sticker book, she found a shoebox that Aunt May had given her.

Since Aunt May had big feet, it was a big box. Once, in school, when they made pinhole cameras out of shoeboxes, the other class had made dioramas. She could make a diorama in the box, with a hole to peek in and a place on the top to let the light in.

I'll make one for Dad, she decided. It's better than just a card.

First she cut the peephole in the front for viewing. The light flap would be on the lid. What could she put inside? What kind of scene?

She stared at the box, but the gray cardboard gave her no ideas. She looked at the dollhouse, but it didn't help either. Then she looked out the window. The maple tree's branches swayed in the wind, the leaves slick with the rain.

Trees. There should be trees in the diorama, that was sure. All different kinds of trees. A forest, with tall pine trees and leafy maples, and silver birches.

The construction-paper pack had only two kinds of green, bright kelly green and a lighter yellow green. But the crayons had a few more tones: dark green, blue-green, grass green. There were brown and black crayons for the trunks and silver for the birch trees.

Soon she had made a dozen different trees and pasted their hinges inside the box. Some looked realistic, others she made up herself. Her favorite was shaped like a giant green gumdrop. It gave her the idea of adding elves.

Elves live in the forest; their homes are inside the trees and in between their roots, Lydia told herself. She drew little people with green clothes and tiny red pointed caps. Then she cut out each one and pasted them in among the trees, peeking out or leaning on a trunk, or even sitting up on a branch.

Above the forest she made a deep blue sky, with two tiny birds flying. But the scene wasn't finished. It needed more color.

From a sheet of stickers that Ivy had traded her, Lydia added flowers. She found stickers of butterflies and a deer to add. As a last touch, she drew a stream meandering through the trees. The elves need a place to swim, she told herself, and water to cook with and wash with. Besides, the sound of the stream will be cheerful.

She placed the cover on top and cut open the light flap. The tiny scene, lit from above, looked magical. It was easy to imagine yourself walking through the woods and meeting an elf. You could sit on the log and talk. You could fish in the stream. The box made you believe it.

Lydia headed downstairs to show Aunt May.

Aunt Connie had come home in the meantime. Lydia showed the box to them both.

"This is so lovely, Lydia," Aunt May said, with genuine delight in her voice. "I've never seen anything like it. Whatever gave you the idea?"

"I saw some dioramas at school once, and there were stuffed ones at the museum that day I got bus sick."

Aunt Connie squinted through the peephole. Then she put on her glasses and tried again. "Good, now I can see. It's the enchanted forest. Oh, I love it. I feel as if I'm really there."

Lydia squirmed at their praise, but she felt happy and proud. It was the nicest thing she'd ever made, and she'd thought of it all by herself.

"I'm going to send it to Dad so he'll have something to look at in the hospital. He's bored. He said so in his letter."

"That's an excellent idea," said Aunt May. "We can send it in the carton we're packing. We bought some new tapes for him to listen to. Your mother said the medicine makes it hard for him to read much. So we're sending tapes of books."

Aunt Connie was peering into the box again. "I wonder . . . have you thought of a fair project yet, Lydia?"

"No. I tried but I couldn't think of anything that wasn't boring or too hard or just too ordinary."

"Well, I think you should make some more of these boxes. This is so delightful! You have an eye for color and detail. It's beautifully made, too. You can enter in the arts and crafts category."

Lydia considered it. What scenes could she do? This one had just flowed out of her head. She hardly even thought about it.

"I don't know if I can think up any more."

Connie brushed her objection aside. "Nonsense. Use your imagination. Use the books you've read. Use your memory. You can make scenes from stories, if you like. Cinderella and her fairy godmother. Red Riding Hood and the wolf. The little mermaid."

Lydia smiled, catching her aunt's enthusiasm. She could do it. With each story mentioned, a scene came to mind.

"I want to get more paper. And stickers too, and toothpicks. It's a good idea. Thanks! But I still want to send this one to Dad."

"I'll pack it in the carton," Aunt May said. "Why don't you write a letter to go with it? I'm going to mail it tomorrow."

"Do you have any more shoeboxes?" Lydia asked them both.

"Check the upstairs closets and the boiler room in the cellar. I'm sure there are a few lying around ready to be transformed. You can use the ribbon box too, and the gift-wrap box. They're in the cellar next to the holiday decorations," Aunt May told her.

Aunt Connie was heading upstairs to change. "I'll check my closet right now," she said.

Lydia went down to the basement in search of odds and ends. She finally had a project for the fair! And she had two more weeks to get ready. Maybe she'd win a prize. Maybe her mother would be there and she'd win a prize and make her happy.

I'm so glad it rained, she thought.

The rain stopped the next day, and sky-blue posters with red and yellow Ferris wheels in the center appeared all over town announcing the August fair. They hung on the door to the children's library, on the boathouse at the lake, on the telephone poles at the railroad station and by the movie theater.

Lydia traced the spokes of the Ferris wheel on the boathouse poster. " 'Rides, booths, contests, fireworks. Fun for all ages,' " she read aloud.

"Last year I won a giant rabbit," Emily said.

"Your father won the rabbit," Ivy corrected her.

"My father won it throwing baseballs but he gave it to me."

"Well, he wouldn't want it for himself, would he?" said Ivy. "A giant pink bunny on his bed would look pretty weird."

Lydia giggled at the thought of Mr. Mott sleeping with his arms around a stuffed animal.

"My mother will get here just in time for the fair," Lydia realized, counting the days on her fingers. "She's coming a week from Friday."

"Are you finished with your project?" Emily asked.

"Not yet. I have two boxes to go."

"Can we see them?" asked Ivy.

"When I'm done."

Lydia had finished three boxes so far, but she still kept adding to them, finding new ideas for little extra things. A kitten or a mouse sticker for a kitchen scene; a doily to use for an apron or a bonnet.

The scene from "Cinderella" was her favorite. Cinderella was crying by the fireplace. In the center of the room, the fairy godmother had just appeared, looking slightly dazed, as if magic travel left her a little disoriented. A pumpkin as big as a footstool sat by the door. Lydia had made it out of orange Play-Doh, and she'd used shiny gold foil for the fairy godmother's gown and matchsticks for the logs in the fireplace.

The scenes from "Snow White" and from "The Three Bears" still weren't finished. Tired of making the inside of rooms, she'd tried to think of an outdoor scene from "The Three Bears" that would show the bears and Goldilocks both. Finally she decided to have the bears' house in one corner, with Goldilocks peeping in the window, while on the other side of the box, the bears would be going off into the forest for their stroll.

"I'm going to work on them every night this week. But I've got to get more stuff."

"I'll go downtown with you," Emily offered. "Are you going to the five-and-ten?"

Lydia nodded.

"Drat!" said Ivy. She'd been saying that ever since she read it in a book. "I can't go. My mom's taking me to the mall to get new sneakers for school. I'd rather go with you." She looked at her sneakers, once pink, now gray. "When I was younger, I used to get excited about new sneakers."

Lydia nodded. "Me too. I used to beg for purple sneakers with Velcro, or sneakers with elephant faces on the front."

Emily joined in. "One time I saw sneakers that played 'From the Halls of Montezuma.' They were green and brown, like army clothes, and the song played when you pushed the heel."

Mrs. Ames wouldn't change her plans, so Lydia and Emily headed downtown on bikes by themselves. Lydia rode Aunt Connie's old three-speed. It wasn't as shiny as her regular bike but it rode smoothly and it was one more thing that made her feel at home.

The five-and-ten contained hardly anything that cost only five or ten cents anymore. The gumball machine at the front took a nickel, and the cardboard fortune cards cost a dime. Everything else was more than a quarter.

Lydia and Emily walked to the back where the arts and crafts supplies were kept. The old wooden floor, buckled with age, was as wavy as the lake on a windy day.

"It would be great to roller-skate in here," Emily said, following Lydia through the store.

As she spotted good finds, Lydia dropped them in the shopping basket: gummed stars, a new glue stick, colored cardboard, origami paper with designs on it.

Emily bought a tube of plastic bubble goop.

"Why don't you let me see the boxes?" Emily pestered.

"I'll show you as soon as I've finished."

"But why can't I see the ones you've finished already?"

Lydia shrugged. She didn't want anyone to see them before the fair. What if they weren't any good? If she lost her nerve, she wouldn't enter them and then she wouldn't have a chance at any prize and her aunts would be disappointed.

"Enter for the fun of it," Aunt May kept saying. But it was serious to Lydia. If you work hard at something and then people don't like it, you feel as if your best wasn't any good.

Emily stopped begging. They rode home and played badminton.

"I'm so glad my mother's coming," Lydia said when they were taking a break, sucking on orange-juice ice pops from the Motts' freezer.

"Why didn't she come sooner?" Emily asked.

"She had to work and go visit my dad. I'm going to show her how I can swim. We'll swim out to the raft together. She won't believe I can go that far," Lydia said.

Emily nodded.

By the next Friday, Lydia was so excited that she had trouble concentrating on her swimming lesson. Her teacher had to remind her over and over to keep her face in the water as she swam. After lunch Lydia put on her dress and combed her hair neatly. She had even polished her white sandals.

At the airport Lydia and her aunts waited at the end of a long corridor. As each plane arrived, a stream of people walked toward them.

"I can't see her." Lydia hopped on one foot and then the other impatiently.

Finally she spotted her mother in the crowd. Her hair was cut very short and she was even thinner than Lydia remembered. Maybe it was the bag she carried over her shoulder that made her seem stooped over, or maybe she was just tired.

"Mommy!" Lydia threw her arms around her mother's neck and kissed her, breathing in her lemony summer perfume.

Her mother squeezed her tight and grinned. "Have I missed your hugs!"

"Hello, Janie." Aunt May kissed her cheek and took the bag off her shoulder.

"Oh, it's good to have you here at last," said Aunt Connie.

"It's good to be here," said Lydia's mother. She linked her arm through Lydia's as they walked to the luggage area.

Her suitcase finally appeared on the shiny carousel, and Lydia managed to pull it off all by herself. Aunt May carried it to the car and put it in back. Lydia and her mother sat together in the backseat. All the way home, her mother talked rapid-fire about Lydia's father, the hospital, the doctors. She spoke quietly but so quickly, as if trying to get it all out so she would be done with it.

The car pulled into the driveway of the old house. "It's exactly the way I remember it," Lydia's mother said.

"We've put you in the front room next to Lyddie," said Aunt Connie. "She's in your old room, but it's her room now."

Lydia smiled to herself. It was *her* room now.

After her mother changed into shorts, Lydia showed her the garden.

"I do the weeding and I planted some stuff myself, peas and string beans, and these squash hills."

She paused by the apple tree to check her monogrammed apples. They'd grown much bigger and hung heavily from the branch. One was beginning to redden. The others were still green. With the tape covering the skin, Lydia couldn't tell what the monogram looked like.

Jane swatted a mosquito that had landed on her calf. "First bite! That didn't take long. They want a taste of pale city blood, I guess." Her mother held out an arm to compare with Lydia's. "Look how tan you are!"

Her arm was pale as skim milk against Lydia's freckled tan.

"I didn't get outside much this summer, but I'll make up for it now. Let's go to the beach tomorrow and stay all day."

They circled back toward the kitchen door. On the porch, her mother stretched out on a lounge chair and settled her head back against the cushion.

"Want a glass of lemonade or some iced tea?" Lydia asked.

"Iced tea sounds delicious. Thanks, sweetie," she answered with her eyes closed.

By the time Lydia returned with the glass, her mother had fallen asleep. She wandered back inside and told her aunts, who were starting to make dinner.

"She's worn out," said Aunt Connie. "Poor chick.

Completely worn out from everything she's had to deal with. I'm glad she's finally here with us. We can help her now."

"Maybe she doesn't want to be helped," suggested Aunt May. "Lots of people like managing on their own."

Aunt Connie snorted. "Just because you're a stubborn old crow doesn't mean everyone insists on total independence."

Aunt May chuckled. "I like to solve my own problems. Then I have no one to blame but myself. I think Jane's doing a fine job."

"Certainly she is. But she's exhausted and she needs a rest."

"A rest, yes. Advice, no."

"Goodness. You sound as if I'm an interfering old biddy."

"So I'm a crow and you're a biddy. A pair of birdbrains is more like it," May joked, making Connie laugh in spite of herself. "Just let her have a vacation. That's what she came for, to rest and see her daughter. Right?"

She gave Lydia a pat on the back.

"Right?" May asked again.

"Right," said Lydia.

DIVING IN THE DEEP END

Jane slept until ten the next morning. Then, out at the lake, she fell asleep on the blanket before Lydia could even show how she could swim.

"Let her sleep," said Aunt May. "You can show her when she wakes up. There's plenty of time. We're staying all day."

Lydia read while her mother slept. She was in the middle of the third book in the series she'd started during the rainy week. The pig keeper's adventures had become more exciting and scarier. Now he had some friends along on the journey: a princess, a musician and a strange, furry creature who liked food, rhymes and funny words.

Finally Jane opened her eyes and, squinting against the sun, smiled at her daughter. "Did I sleep long?"

"Half an hour, I guess."

"I feel baked."

She propped herself up on her elbows and looked at the lake. It was a deep blue, with occasional clouds reflected on the smooth surface.

"Want to come in for a swim?" she asked.

Lydia popped up like a piece of toast. Jane got to her feet more slowly, and stretched her arms toward the sky, yawning still. She followed Lydia down to the water.

Lydia splashed right in. Jane waded in more cautiously, her arms wrapped around her middle.

"Let's swim to the raft," Lydia suggested.

"Can you really swim that far?"

"Sure. I've done it before." She swam out once with Ivy, and she'd had to roll over and float on her back three times each way, just to catch her breath.

But this time she tried to swim slowly and smoothly. She stayed right behind her mother, who checked back often. By the time they reached the raft, Lydia was tired, but she hadn't run out of breath or gotten scared.

They had the raft to themselves.

"Feels just like a sauna out here," Jane said, patting the sun-baked boards. She lay on her back, eyes closed. "Don't let me fall asleep again, Lyddie. I'll be red as a tomato. You are really a good swimmer now, you know that? You kept right up with me, and it wasn't any baby stroke! The crawl, all the way out. I'm impressed.''

Lydia lay beside her, watching the clouds move across the sky, slow as giant turtles. She smiled at the compliment.

''Wait until your father sees you.''

''When can I show him?'' If her father could come swimming, Lydia knew for sure that he was going to get better.

''There's a chance that he'll be home at the beginning of September. But it's not a sure thing.''

Lydia frowned. It was never a sure thing. That proved it. He probably wasn't getting better. They just wouldn't tell her.

''When can I see him?''

''As soon as we get back we'll go right over to the hospital. He loves the magic box you sent him. He says that every time he's discouraged, he looks inside. It's his magic charm. He says the magic will make him well. I think he really believes that. How did you make it?''

''I got a shoebox and made the trees and then I just started putting in more things.''

''And you thought of it all by yourself?''

''I thought of that one all by myself, then Aunt Connie thought I should make some for the fair and enter them in the arts and crafts division.''

''So are you?''

"Yes. I made five boxes. Each one has a fairy tale inside. I entered them as a set."

"When can I see them?"

"At the fair."

"And when will they tell the winners?"

"I don't know. I forgot to ask Aunt Connie. She entered some fudge. And Aunt May entered her giant tomatoes and her eggplants."

"I can't wait to see the boxes. I never knew you were so artistic, Lyddie."

"I didn't know either. It just popped out."

They lay on the raft quietly for a while, feeling it sway gently in the water. Lydia imagined she was floating on a lily pad like Thumbelina. That would have been a good story for a box.

"Lyddie, would you like to learn how to dive?" her mother asked.

"Dive?"

"Sure. It's not hard. You're such a good swimmer now. You could easily learn. You just have to get the angle right and keep your nerve up. But if you swam all the way out here, you've got plenty of nerve."

"Okay. I'll try it."

"Good." Jane was already on her feet. "This is perfect. There's nobody around to make us feel silly."

Lydia liked the way she said "us."

"Stand at the side and curl your toes over the edge."

Lydia walked to the side, feeling the raft dip as

they both stood on the same side. The water was very close.

"Bend over and put your arms up by your ears. Point your fingers right down at the water." Jane bent Lydia almost in two.

"Good. That's it. Now bend your knees and push off, and you'll glide right in."

Jane gave her a helpful little shove and in she went. It was more of a crash than a glide. Water went up her nose and in her mouth. She came up spluttering.

"Great!" Jane called.

Lydia somehow found her way to the ladder and crawled back onto the raft, grateful for a solid surface.

"I don't think I did it right," she said.

"Try it again," Jane insisted.

Reluctantly, Lydia let herself be folded, prodded and pushed off one more time. The water didn't go up her nose because she kept her chin tucked just as Jane had instructed. It still wasn't a glide. But it wasn't a crash either.

"Once more," Jane urged her. "Tuck your chin. Keep your arms straight. Bend your knees and push off as slowly and as smoothly as you can. You'll flow right in. You'll glide like a minnow."

This time she slid easily into the water.

"You did it! You really did it," Jane called, clapping her hands.

Lydia tried it again and again, and each time her

dives got smoother. Finally her mother said, "You'd better rest a bit. We should swim back soon."

But as they were getting ready to swim back, her aunts swam out, and Lydia showed off her diving again.

"I would never believe this is the same girl who couldn't swim a month ago," said Aunt Connie.

Lydia grinned, and dived off again. She could hardly believe it herself. She was diving in the deep end of the lake and it wasn't even scary. It was fun!

THE AUGUST FAIR

The fair opened the next day. Even Aunt May was excited. "I love the sound of the carousel."

"Yes, and the Ferris wheel at night," Jane said. "The lights on the other rides glow in the dark and you can see the stars too. From the top you can see the steeple of the church on the green, all lit up against the sky. When I was a kid, I rode it every year."

"Can I come with you?" Lydia asked.

"Only if you promise you won't rock too much."

"I won't rock."

"It's a date. How're those cookies coming?"

Lydia was baking cookies for the fair picnic. Jane was frying chicken. Aunt Connie was making her famous coleslaw and two pies, peach and blueberry.

"I'm the official taster and the general general," Aunt May said without a hint of embarrassment. "Troops, your travel instructions: We'll leave about one. That gives us some time before supper to check out the exhibits and join some contests, time for our picnic, and lots of time for after supper."

"When are the contests, Lyddie?" asked Jane. "And which ones did you enter us in?"

"Four-thirty, I think. We're signed up for the three-legged race, the potato sack relay, the wheelbarrow race and the raw egg run."

"Good thing they're before dinner. I'd hate to do all that on a full stomach."

"Mrs. Mott asked us to sit with them for the picnic," said Aunt May. "We'll all share desserts. I'm going downstairs to see if I can find the cooler."

That night, when Jane came in to tuck Lydia into bed, she paused by the dollhouse. She ran her finger along the curved back of the old couch, and picked up one of the old-fashioned lamps.

"There's something special about this house, isn't there? No matter what you add or move around, it seems to stay the same." She picked up the tiny father doll and looked at him with a soft smile. "I can't imagine anything sad happening to this family, can you?"

"They have adventures," Lydia said. "We took them climbing on cliffs and the children had to be rescued."

"Adventures, yes. I gave them adventures too. But those were just scrapes, not real catastrophes. Except one time when our yellow cat took the little girl. I finally found her under the sofa. She wasn't chewed really, just damp. I guess if a doll ever really got lost that would be a truly sad thing."

She put the little father doll back in the house, setting him gently on the sofa beside his wife.

Jane gave Lydia a hug and a kiss and turned out the light on the bedstand. Moonlight from the window made the room pale. "Want me to pull the shade down?" she asked Lydia.

"No, I like it this way."

"They say moonlight gives you dreams," her mother said.

"I bet I dream about the fair," Lydia said.

If she dreamed about the fair, she didn't remember it the next morning. She woke for the first time at dawn, shivering in the unexpected cold. She groped for the blanket at the foot of her bed and pulled it up over her shoulders. Only half awake, she snuggled under its comforting woolly weight and drifted back to sleep. She woke again when the teakettle whistled downstairs.

"Brrr. It's cold," she said to Aunt May, who was greasing the waffle iron.

"Taste of fall. Got to get busy and gather up those seeds and acorns."

Lydia looked out the window at the marigolds with their bright round heads crowded together. Zinnias were still blooming and the geraniums stood tall. Only the petunias were limp from last night's chill.

On the way to the fairgrounds, Jane and the aunts sang every song they could think of that mentioned a fair. May insisted on adding "Take Me Out to the Ball Game" even though the others didn't think it fit.

They parked the car in a rutted field turned parking lot for the day.

"Let's leave everything in the car until the picnic. We don't want to lug stuff around with us," said May.

"Exhibits first," said Jane. "Let's see how Lyddie's boxes did."

In a big building that had once been a barn, tables lined both walls, piled with cakes, cookies, pies and candy, then the vegetables and the fruit, then the sewing and the arts and crafts. Prize ribbons, blue and red and yellow, were pinned or taped on the winners. A watermelon as big as a pig wore a shiny blue ribbon lying on top. Aunt May's vegetables hadn't won anything.

"Just not big enough," she said with a smile. "Next year I'll try seed frames and start even earlier. That's the trick, I think."

The arts and crafts were down at the end of the

aisle. At first Lydia couldn't find her boxes. Then Jane spotted them in the corner.

"Look, there they are, on the shelf."

Lydia found them finally. She was about to pick up Cinderella and peer in at the little scene when she noticed the ribbon. It was taped to the side of the Three Bears box. A blue ribbon.

"First Prize, Junior Division," she read.

"Congratulations!" said her mother, giving her a hug.

Aunt Connie and Aunt May hugged her too.

She just grinned, not knowing what to say. She'd never won anything before.

Jane was busy peering into each scene. "Look at the details in this one," she said, handing the Snow White box to Aunt Connie. "I still can't get over how magical these are. You make a little world in each one."

"And you said you didn't have anything special about you," Aunt May teased.

Lydia and Jane didn't win any of the races later. They stumbled over each other's feet in the three-legged race and their wheelbarrow kept coming apart even though Jane tried to hold on to Lydia's legs. They laughed so hard that tears made tiny lines on their dusty faces.

Mrs. Mott and Emily won the egg race. But Ivy's egg landed on her mother's foot.

"Ick!" said Mrs. Ames, wiping egg yolk off her toes.

After the contests were over and the prizes had been distributed, Jane and Lydia walked slowly toward the picnic area with their arms around each other.

Aunt Connie had spread out two blankets on a soft grassy spot, near a big beech tree. Mrs. Mott had set out her family's blankets nearby and so had Ivy's mother. More and more families wandered onto the field until it looked like a village of blankets.

Jane flopped on her stomach and sighed. "If I laugh anymore my stomach will split."

Lydia wasn't ready to sit down yet.

"Come and play tag," Ivy said.

Lydia followed her to the other side of the field where there weren't any blankets to avoid. When they returned, the food was spread out and the grown-ups had started to help themselves. She, Emily and Ivy filled their own plates and sat with their backs leaning comfortably against the trunk of the big beech tree.

Lydia listened to the music from the rides. "What ride should we go on first?"

"The Octopus," said Ivy.

"The Wild Mouse," said Emily.

"Save the Ferris wheel for me," Jane called over to Lydia. "We'll go up together when it's dark."

Throughout the meal, people stopped by the blanket to say hello to Jane, old friends from grade school and high school who had heard she was back, May and Connie's friends who wanted to welcome her, even her old boyfriend from college.

"I didn't know Tom still lived here," Jane said to May when the dark-haired man had left.

"Moved back about three years ago to help run his father's practice. The judge retired finally."

The girls were finished eating and anxious to get off to the rides.

"Can I go now?" Lydia asked.

"May I," her mother corrected. "Yes, you may. Want to take a brownie? Oh, wait, you need money for the rides and the booths." She dug around in her pocket and gave Lydia several crumpled bills and some change. "Don't bother with the coin toss. It's impossible to win anything except an ashtray, and nobody here smokes. I'll meet you at the Ferris wheel at nine, okay?"

Lydia nodded and waved goodbye. She had to run to catch up with Emily and Ivy, who were halfway across the field already.

The Octopus's eight legs ended in cup-shaped seats. The girls paid their money, hurried up the ramp and slid into an empty seat together.

"It gets slippery when it twirls around," Ivy warned. "You bump into each other like crazy."

The ride man checked the seats, making sure that each door was firmly shut. Then he stepped into the control booth.

"Hold on tight, everyone," he said through the microphone. "Here we go!"

The music blared and the lights on the Octopus arms blinked on and off as the machine revolved in a slow circle. Gradually the speed increased and the arms began to move up and down as well. Around and up and down at the same time. Just when Lydia thought she could handle this ride after all, the seat itself began to spin around. Ivy shrieked in delight as she slid into Emily, who laughed and tried to brace herself by holding tight to the center handle. Lydia, tossed first right, then left, was too scared to enjoy herself.

"Put out your arms and hold on to the back with both hands," Ivy suggested, guessing from the look on her face that she was frightened.

"And brace your feet against the center post," Emily added.

Lydia did what they said. Once she felt more in control, she began to enjoy herself, and even laughed when the arm flew up and then dropped sharply with no warning. When the ride slowed down and finally stopped, she was willing to go again.

"Let's try some others first. We can come back later," Emily said. "Wild Mouse is next."

The Wild Mouse had tiny cars on a track that zigzagged in and out of a huge piece of cheese. There was only room for two in each car.

"I'll go alone," Ivy offered.

Lydia and Emily squeezed into one car and Ivy climbed into the car behind them.

"Squeak, squeak!" she called. "Watch out for the cat."

The little mouse car climbed the steep rise inch by inch, then whipped around the first corner and shot down the track. Zoom, it raced toward the edge.

"Aaaaah!" Lydia screamed. It looked as if the car would fly right off the track. But just at the last possible second, it turned abruptly to the right and dived down the side, leaving Lydia's stomach behind.

Never, not for one instant, did the mouse slow down, so Lydia had no chance to look at Emily. She just clutched the bar and screamed until the ride ended with a jolt. To her surprise, both Emily and Ivy were grinning.

"That was great!" Emily said. "I like the place where it looks like it's going straight out into the air, and then it turns instead."

Lydia said nothing, but wiped her sweaty hands on her shorts and smoothed her hair back off her face.

Next they rode the carousel a few times. Never had the old merry-go-round looked so good! The horses went up and down gently, and if you wanted an even tamer ride, you could sit in the coach pulled by tigers.

They each chose an outside horse so they could reach for the ring. Lydia's was black with red silk tassels and a purple saddle. Ivy's horse was white and Emily's was gray. By grabbing the pole and leaning out, Lydia could reach the rings with ease. But she got only silver rings, never brass.

At nine she headed toward the Ferris wheel. Jane stood by the ticket stall, searching the crowd with her eyes.

"Hi, Mom," Lydia said.

"Oh, there you are! I was afraid I'd missed you. I went on the Wild Mouse with May. This is more my speed. Come on, I bought the tickets already."

They stood in line for just a few minutes. The wheel circled smoothly, its little baskets swinging back and forth. Against the dark sky, the colored lights twinkled and the music played continuously, as cheerful as the music on the carousel.

Jane and Lydia waited for the man to wave them forward, then sat down in the basket. As soon as every seat was full, the wheel began to turn, bringing them up to the top, then down the other side. Beneath them, the entire park spread out, with its bursts of color and shrieks of laughter and excitement. Above them, the sky was dark, dotted with stars, quiet and mysterious.

"Look over to the right." Jane pointed. "The moon is rising."

Lydia spotted its round shape threading through the trees.

" 'Who knows if the moon's a balloon,' " Jane

said. "That's what e. e. cummings said. It does look like a balloon, doesn't it?"

The wheel came to a gentle stop, leaving them hanging just below the top.

"Oh good," said Jane. "What a view. Look how tiny the town is, Lyddie. You can see almost to the lake, I think. Don't you love it here?"

Lydia nodded. She loved the old house and her aunts. Eccentric, Mr. Mott called them. Off the center. Not the usual sort. And she loved her friends. They'd made her feel welcome. She loved the town itself with its old trees and big yards, its streets empty enough for games of kickball and hopscotch.

"I wish we could live here, Mom."

"Would you like that?" Jane stared up at the stars.

Lydia nodded.

"Maybe we'll think about it when Daddy's better. It would be lovely to be closer to May and Connie. I miss having family nearby. We'll talk to Daddy about it when we get home."

The wheel began to turn once more. When they reached the bottom, Jane said, "Let's go again." She gave the man two more tickets and they stayed in their seat.

Down below, the fair stretched out like a make-believe land.

"It could be a scene in one of my boxes," Lydia said. "I'll make a fair box for Daddy."

"He could pretend he'd been here with us."

Jane sounded sad. Lydia remembered her own doubts.

"Mom, is Daddy really going to get better?"

Jane squeezed her hand. "I think so, sweetheart. He's trying so hard. The doctors are trying. He's got a good chance, but it's not a sure thing. It never is."

"What will we do if he dies?"

"I don't like to think about it. I don't think it's going to happen, I really don't. Mike wants to live more than anything. He's a fighter."

They sat in silence, holding hands, as the little basket swung gently in the dark. Lydia wanted to ask again, but hesitated. What if he didn't win the fight? Why didn't her mother say what would happen then?

As if she could read her thoughts, Jane continued, "If Daddy doesn't get well, sweetheart, we'll miss him. We'll miss him, but we'll keep on going. We'll figure out what to do, and we'll keep going, right?"

Jane put her arm around Lydia's shoulders and pulled her close. Lydia let herself be cuddled. The fear gradually faded.

"I want him to get better, Mom."

"We all do. Next week you can see him and tell him yourself. He's so anxious to see you."

The ride was over. They hadn't even noticed that the wheel had stopped turning and now was moving in little starts, letting off passengers from each basket. Their basket landed at the bottom and the driver helped them step down.

Walking into the crowd, Lydia turned to her mother. "It's nice here at Christmas," she said with a grin.

Jane laughed and gave her a hug. "I know it is. Is this a hint? Okay, maybe we can all come for Christmas this time."

"I hope so," Lydia said.

On the last night of their visit, Aunt May and Aunt Connie planned a special dinner.

"Fresh picked vegetables from the garden, lobsters, butter and sugar corn, and blueberry pie with ice cream," Aunt Connie said.

They ate outside at the picnic table, but Aunt May covered it with a lace tablecloth and set the places with Grandma's old silver and cut-glass goblets. In the center she lined up a row of tall white candles. It was already twilight when they sat down to eat. The candles lit the table and made the silver shine.

"I feel so elegant," Jane said. "All we need is a violinist to serenade us."

"I'll whistle," Lydia offered.

"Somehow I doubt if it will have the same atmosphere," said Aunt May. "Just concentrate on your lobster."

At the beginning of the summer, May had taught her how to break the claws and scoop out the meat.

"I wish we could stay longer," Jane said.

"You'll be back," said May.

"Try for Christmas," Connie said. "It would be wonderful to have everyone together for a big celebration. We can have turkey. Or a goose, that would be fun. A Christmas goose and plum pudding." Connie pointed at Lydia with her fork. "And you can make cookies and string the popcorn."

Lydia smiled, remembering last year's Christmas. Caroling with Emily and Ivy. Building snow families and going sledding. But this time maybe her father would be along, and they could ride the big toboggan together.

"I promise, we'll try to make it. There's nothing I'd like more," Jane said. "To have Mike get better and come here for the holidays—that's my idea of heaven."

While the grown-ups talked, Lydia stared out at the yard and the garden. It was dark now, and the line between the garden and the trees blurred. The moon gave a little light, but the stars outshone it. Since she'd missed the first star, she changed the words of the rhyme: Star light, star bright, all the stars I see tonight, I wish I may, I wish I might, have the wish I wish tonight.

The next morning Emily and Ivy were sitting on the front step when Lydia carried her suitcase out to the car.

"Surprise! Your aunts said we could come to the airport," Emily said.

Ivy was hiding a package behind her back. Lydia spied one on the step behind Emily too.

"Wait just a second. I'll be right down again," she said.

Her backpack sat on the chair where she had left it. In the front pocket she'd packed the swimmer's card awarded on the last day of lessons. She was in the intermediate class now.

She'd also packed her aunts' going-away present, a jigsaw puzzle of elves in a snowy forest.

"It reminded us of the magic woods that you sent your father, and of the conversation we had the night we did the mystery puzzle together," Aunt Connie said when they gave it to her.

"You've figured out how special you are, I think," Aunt May added. "And if you ever forget, you just give us a call and we'll remind you."

She took a last look at the dollhouse. Everyone was comfortably seated in the living room together, even the cook and the baby. They would wait for her return. She pretended to turn on the old-fashioned radio so the dolls would have music to listen to while they waited.

With her backpack over one shoulder, she went quickly downstairs and managed to slip out the back door without being seen. She had one last errand to do in the garden.

Back at the front of the house, the car was packed and her mother, her aunts and Emily and Ivy were standing in the driveway waiting to pile into the car.

"Where were you?" Jane asked.

"I took a last look at the garden."

"Everything's packed. Even the magic boxes."

The three sisters sat in front, Jane in the middle and May at the wheel. The three friends sat in back. No one talked much on the way to the airport.

At the ticket counter, they checked their bags, but Lydia kept her knapsack on. Then they all went to the gate to wait for the boarding announcement.

Finally Emily brought out the present she'd been trying to keep out of sight. "We brought you going-away presents. Open Ivy's first."

Lydia unwrapped the square package. It was a box of notecards, with a different-colored crayon on the front of each.

"So you can write to us," Ivy said. "Now open Emily's."

It was also square, but heavier.

Lydia untied the ribbon and slipped off the wrapping paper.

"An address book! I never had one."

"Look inside," Emily said.

Lydia flipped through the pages and stopped when she spotted some writing. Emily's address, Leo's and Johnny Ringer's, Ivy's, her aunts', had each been printed carefully under the right letter.

"Thank you!" Lydia said. "I have something for you too. And for you," she said to her aunts.

"You imp!" said Aunt Connie.

"Everybody close your eyes," she ordered. "Except you, Mom."

She reached into her knapsack. "Put out your hands." Into each outstretched pair of hands she placed a monogrammed apple. In the center of each apple was a pale letter. I for Ivy, E for Emily, M for May and C for Connie.

"Boarding Flight 731 at Gate 9," the loudspeaker voice said.

"That's us," said Jane.

Jane hugged her sisters and picked up her bag.

Lydia hugged her aunts. "Thank you for having me."

"We loved it," said May.

"It would've been so dull without you," said Aunt Connie. "Hurry back! I'm counting on Christmas."

"Goodbye, Lydia," said Emily. "I promise I'll write."

"Me too," said Ivy. "You can write to us together."

Lydia put on her backpack and followed her mother down the aisle. Before passing through the door to the ramp, she looked back and waved, wanting one last glimpse of the four people who had made this summer special. Aunt May, tall and thin as ever; Aunt Connie waving with a sad smile on her face; Emily and Ivy, standing with their arms around each other's shoulders, waving.

"I'll be back," called Lydia.

CHRISTINE MCDONNELL graduated from Barnard College and Columbia University School of Library Service. She has worked as a teacher and children's librarian, as well as a writer of children's books. She currently teaches at the Pierce School in Brookline, Massachusetts. She lives with her family in Boston.

DIANE DE GROAT is the illustrator of many books for children, including *Chasing Trouble* (Viking) and *Toad Food & Measle Soup*, by Christine McDonnell (Puffin). She received her Bachelor of Fine Arts degree from Pratt Institute. Ms. de Groat lives in Yonkers, New York, with her husband and daughter.